"Emma, you're

"No. I had no idea." Which was a lie. Emma was very much aware of the sexual tension running between her and Kyle. It was almost tangible, especially when they were mostly naked, standing only inches apart.

"You are. And I most definitely can keep a secret, so if anything else happens here today, you can be sure it will never be mentioned at the office. Or ever, for that matter, if that's what you want."

"What could happen?"

"This." Kyle closed the gap between them.

Her eyes fluttered shut as his mouth covered hers in a deep, tantalizing kiss. *Wowsa*. Kyle's lips teased over hers with just the right amount of pressure and finesse, his touch confident and smooth but not arrogant.

Kyle had most definitely surprised her. In the sexiest way possible.

Dear Reader,

Double Exposure is the launch of my series From All Angles and my very first Harlequin Blaze book! Before I sold my first book in 2002 it was always my dream to write for Harlequin Blaze, and so I am very excited that three years ago I reconnected with editor Wanda Ottewell on a conference cruise to Cozumel and the wheels starting turning for a new series. Sun, margaritas and good company make fabulous inspirations.

For years I had wanted to write about a photographer who specializes in mass nudes (I figured the humor and sexiness in that situation was a no-brainer!) and *Double Exposure* features a couple of reporters who are on the scene at the shoot. Sometimes a whole lot more than skin is revealed when the clothes come off.

I hope you enjoy my take on photography, and I'm thrilled to finally be part of the amazing stories and writers who make Harlequin Blaze so exciting!

Happy reading,

Erin McCarthy

Double Exposure

New York Times Bestselling Author
Erin McCarthy

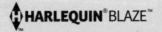

Recycling programs
for this product may
not exist in your area.

ISBN-13: 978-0-373-79808-7

DOUBLE EXPOSURE

Copyright © 2014 by Erin McCarthy

Printed in U.S.A.

HARLEQUIN®
www.Harlequin.com

ABOUT THE AUTHOR

USA TODAY and *New York Times* bestselling author Erin McCarthy sold her first book in 2002 and has since written almost fifty novels and novellas in teen fiction, new adult and adult romance. Erin has a special weakness for tattoos, karaoke, high-heeled boots and martinis. She lives on the shores of Lake Erie in Ohio with her family, her cat and her stylish and well-dressed Chihuahua/terrier mix.

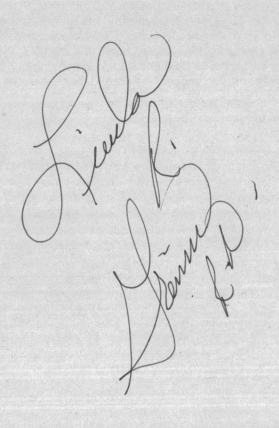

1

"So when do we get naked?"

Emma Gideon shot a look at her coworker Kyle Hadley and tried not to hurt him. He didn't make it easy to refrain from violence, standing there looking all casual, ready to peel off his shirt at a single word. Nothing about this photo shoot intimidated him, whereas Emma wanted to crawl into a hole and bury herself under heavy fleece blankets at the thought of taking off her clothes in front of other people.

This was career dedication. But as she stood in the parking lot of an abandoned warehouse with two hundred other people prepared to strip down to their underwear, she wasn't sure securing an interview with the famed photographer Ian Bainbridge was worth this level of discomfort.

"If you do it too soon, the organizers will kick you out, so keep your pants on, please." Emma sidled a look at Kyle's jeans, as if she could tell anything other than that he was muscular. She already knew that. She'd noticed it every single day since he'd joined the newspaper staff twenty-three months and one week ago, three months and fifteen days after she had been hired. Not that she was counting. "Are you wearing boxers? You're supposed to wear underwear. If you're not, they'll kick you out." Aware of how nervous and frantic she sounded, she clapped her mouth shut.

"You're very concerned with me getting tossed out." He adjusted the baseball cap on his head. "I appreciate how badly you want me to stick around."

Emma rolled her eyes. The truth was she'd rather be sharing this story with a rabid dog than with Kyle. Though she wasn't convinced there was much difference between the two. Kyle just smiled more than a disease-ridden mutt. But "dog" definitely described him.

As if to prove her point, he smirked at her and pulled the waistband of his jeans down, revealing taut abdominal muscles and the elastic of his tight black briefs. "But yes, I'm wearing underwear, which I don't mind getting ruined with body paint, per the instructions. I can follow rules."

Somehow Emma doubted that. She had worked with Kyle at the newspaper since that fateful day her boss had hired him, and Kyle seemed to think that charm usurped rules on a regular basis. If he just smiled, it didn't matter if he turned his piece in three hours late. What burned her butt was that it seemed to work for him. She would have been fired five times over if she pulled the stunts he did.

Then again, she wasn't a hot guy who had all the women in the office drooling over him. Their editor was a divorced woman, and Kyle was single and always up for a good time. There was no getting around it, as much as Emma would like to pretend otherwise. Her own personal reaction to him was frustrating in the extreme. She liked to pride herself on her self-control and focus. She was a career woman, driven and sensible. Yet she was like any other female when Kyle walked into the room—weak in the knees and warm between the thighs. It was infuriating. She sympathized with every teenage boy who was at the mercy of his hormones because her reaction to Kyle was just ridiculous.

Now she was going to be mostly nude in a group photo shoot with him. Fabulous.

"I don't care if you stay or not," she told him, "but Claire won't be thrilled if you get tossed out on your ass." His very fine ass, which Emma was afraid she wouldn't be able to resist staring at once he removed his jeans. "I'd rather the focus of this story be my stellar reporting, not your antics."

She might be only a features writer for the Life & Style section of the *Daily Journal,* but she took it seriously. Working on a Sunday like this was a matter of course for her, though usually it wasn't under quite these unusual circumstances. But the only reason she was even joining the actual shoot was because otherwise reporters were restricted solely to the parking lot. Nor was anyone allowed access to the photographer, Ian Bainbridge, and Emma was determined to get at least a word or two with him.

Heralded as the next big thing in group nude photography, Ian was traveling from city to city shooting mass groups of volunteers who he arranged artistically to blend in to whatever environment he had chosen, in order to make a statement. For this particular shoot, he had landed in northeast Ohio and had chosen the crumbling warehouse. It figured. He couldn't choose somewhere attractive, like the lakeshore or the botanical gardens. But Emma reasoned that those places didn't resonate with angsty photographers quite the same way.

So far there hadn't been any sight of Ian, just a slew of security guards patrolling the perimeter and preventing outsiders from snapping pictures with their cell phones. A tent had been set up as a further barrier, and inside participants were being sprayed with body paint and then funneled directly into the dilapidated warehouse. It was actually well-organized and efficient, which meant that any minute now Emma would in fact be forced to take off her jeans and T-shirt, which made her palms sweat. Naked alone, in the shower, was fine. Naked with a man was, well, necessary for the positive outcome that resulted from it. Naked with two hundred strangers? Not okay.

It wasn't that she was a prude. She was just modest. There was nothing wrong with that and Kyle wasn't going to make her feel bad about it.

"My antics? Gee, Mom, I'll be good, I promise. We'll have a swell time." He gave her a broad cheesy smile and swung his arms back and forth.

His sarcasm was not appreciated. Okay, so maybe she was a teeny bit prudish. Or maybe it was just irritating that Kyle hit on every woman between the ages of twenty-four and fifty in the office yet had never once flirted with her. Wasn't she flirtworthy? Not that she would ever consider dating him, not in a million, trillion years, but it would be nice if he tried.

Though why she was thinking about any of that was a mystery to her. She needed to focus on finding Ian. Not on Kyle.

"Besides, Claire won't care. She didn't want two of us on this story, anyway."

That was news to her. "Then why are you here?"

Kyle touched her elbow and directed her into the line outside the tent, where everyone was queuing to be processed. "I think we're supposed to be here. I've seen Ian Bainbridge's work before. I thought it would be cool to be a part of it. I like that he makes a bold statement." Kyle winked at her. "Besides, it's a chance to get naked in public and not get arrested. How often does an opportunity like that come up?"

Emma tossed her blond hair over her shoulder. It was too long and she needed a trim, but she had kept it out of a ponytail this morning because she had thought it would make her feel less naked having hair around her shoulders. The logic seemed flawed in retrospect since her breasts would be totally bare, but she was desperate, quaking in her ballet flats from fear. She wasn't sure what exactly she was afraid of, but she had been less uncomfortable getting a root canal. Maybe she needed anesthetic for this, too. Emma sighed.

"You're a freak," she told him. "People are not supposed to roll around naked together."

He raised an eyebrow. "Really? That's news to everyone I know who's having sex."

Okay, so that wasn't exactly what she had meant. Emma flushed, aware that the line they stood in was gradually moving closer and closer to the entrance of the tent. Where she would have to remove her clothes. Otherwise known as the Panic Room. There were only about eight people in front of her now. "You know what I meant! It's not normal to put two hundred naked people together in a warehouse."

"This isn't a mass orgy. It's art. Which is precisely why Bainbridge does it—Americans are both fascinated and made squeamish by nudity. That's the angle I'm taking on my piece. Claire said I could write a column about the oversexualization of commercial products like movies and advertising, in contrast to the moral restrictions on art that still exist."

Wonderful.

Somehow, Kyle had managed to find an angle that was more in-depth than what Emma was planning while making her sound like a total wet blanket. She had been hoping to score an interview with the photographer himself and question him about his recent run-ins with a stalker. The identity of the person who had been vandalizing his shoot locations and causing damages and loss of time seemed to be personally targeting Ian for his art, and Emma was hoping for an angle that would tie his recent run-ins to the new anti-stalker laws. But that was a big fat *if.* Most likely in the end she would be doing a write-up of the actual event. While Kyle wrote a well-researched opinion article.

At that moment, Emma wasn't sure she could possibly dislike him more. "It sounds obvious," she sniffed. What else was she supposed to say? That he was smarter than she was? She would choke on those words before they came out of her mouth.

She worked her tail off at the paper, and had sacrificed the majority of her social life to get ahead, while Kyle did the minimum. Yet who got more bylines every week?

It wasn't fair.

She was more determined than ever to snag two minutes with Ian Bainbridge.

But first she had to get naked.

"Waiver," an older woman barked at her as they approached the entrance of the tent.

Pulling the model release out of her pocket, Emma handed it to her with sweaty hands, chewing on her bottom lip. She wondered if she could lose Kyle when they were getting their bodies painted. This day might be a lot less humiliating and awful if she didn't have to spend it with her confident, sexy coworker.

"Everything looks good," the woman said briskly, putting a plastic band around her wrist. "You're going to go in this line to the right. You'll be green."

"Green?" Emma looked suspiciously in the direction she'd been pointed to. There were five people in line, two peeling off their pants, two wearing nothing but underwear. The one woman's enormous breasts were just out there for anyone to see. The first person, an older man, was having his sagging belly spray-painted an emerald green.

Yikes.

"Green paint. You're going to be green. Get a move on. You're holding up the line." She gave Emma a look of impatience.

"What about me?" Kyle asked behind her. "Do I get green, too? I'm having an Incredible Hulk fantasy here. My childhood dreams come true."

The woman, who had just been brisk and unimpressed with Emma, now smiled and tittered in delight. "We're supposed to go every other person, but I suppose I could make an exception for you."

Emma rolled her eyes.

Kyle winked at the dragon masquerading as a volunteer. "Thanks, doll. I owe you."

Doll? Was he for real?

But then Emma's irritation at Kyle's powers of persuasion evaporated when the guy in front of her said, "Here's your bag for your clothes and your number so you can reclaim them. When you're ready, hand the bag to Jane here and get in the paint line."

Emma took the bag and number he shoved at her, but then she just stood stock-still, gulping. She couldn't do this. She couldn't take her clothes off with all these people milling around. Granted, no one was looking at her. No one cared. They were all treating their partially nude bodies like this was an everyday occurrence. Making her feel even more self-conscious that she was self-conscious. She stood, palms sweating, heart racing, breath coming in short, frantic bursts.

Suddenly Kyle touched her elbow. "Hey. You don't have to do this if you don't want to, you know. You can still write the story without actually participating."

Given that bile was doing an army crawl up her throat, Emma couldn't speak, but she nodded gratefully. Kyle's face was remarkably sympathetic, all traces of teasing gone from his voice. He was right. She didn't have to do this. If she wasn't comfortable getting her bare breasts sprayed the color of a leprechaun by a total stranger, that didn't make her a prude. It made her modest and meant she had chosen the correct career path. Stripper or Hooters waitress were not going to be successful ventures for her and she was okay with that. She would just do a nice feature on the photo shoot. Hell, maybe being clothed would actually give her better opportunities to spot the photographer. It wasn't like she could really interview him from within a sea of nude bodies. She'd seen enough to do a respectable write-up.

That settled, Emma sighed in relief. Kyle gave her a reassuring smile, then stepped forward, peeling his shirt off. She caught a close-up glimpse of his rippling back muscles and the sexy little divot in the small of his back before she turned, feeling voyeuristic and suddenly outrageously turned on. Time to look away from that.

Only to come face-to-face with a woman behind her who had already stripped down to a pair of white cotton bikini panties. Before she could avert her gaze, Emma saw that the woman had the scars of a double mastectomy on her chest. "Oh! Sorry," she said, mortified, feeling like she had been caught staring, when in reality it had been all of a three-second glance.

But the woman just gave her a warm smile. "You're fine. They have us crammed in here like sardines, but I imagine it's only about to get worse. Glad I remembered my deodorant this morning."

Emma smiled back weakly. "True. But I don't think I'm going to… I think maybe I need to…" She wasn't sure how to express her discomfort, nor was she entirely sure why she was so uncomfortable.

"Not your thing, huh?" Twisting her dark hair into a makeshift bun, the woman said, "I don't think this would have been something I would have done in my twenties, either. But now it's like what the hell. I like this photographer's message—that we're people, not machines or corporations." She gestured to her chest. "Or pharmaceutical or insurance companies. Human beings, in imperfect packages."

Emma bit her lip. "You're right. I was just raised by

a mother who emphasized modesty because my grandfather lived with us. It feels unnatural to me." She had
often thought her mother was big on modesty, too, because she had been worried Emma would turn out the
way she had—knocked up at eighteen, and a single
parent by twenty. Whatever her reasons, the end result was they had kept it on in the Gideon household,
and Emma was not comfortable with multiple people
getting naked together.

Surely she wasn't the only one who felt that way, but
she supposed all her comrades in covering up would
naturally have stayed far away from this event.

"I totally understand," the woman said. "I was,
too. But I think this illustrates that we're really run by
our biology, aren't we? From hunger to sex to disease.
We're already controlled by our bodies, so let's not let
corporations control us, too. Let's liberate ourselves."

Emma had never really given much thought to her
body and how it controlled her. She glanced over her
shoulder to Kyle. Except when Kyle was around. Then
it definitely controlled her. Her desire had a vicelike
grip on her nipples while her lust lobbied between her
legs for a free market.

"You're right," she told the woman, suddenly feeling energized and determined. "Thanks. I want to feel
liberated." She no longer wanted to be the boring office workaholic who couldn't even get a second glance
from Kyle, the serial flirt. She didn't want to be Corporate Emma, cell phone and sensible pumps included,
all the time. Sometimes she wanted to be Easy Breezy
Emma, who had a social life and got laid.

So she took a deep breath. And peeled off her
T-shirt.

Kyle turned, a grin on his face, slapping his baseball cap back on his head. "Hey, Em, look at me—"

She popped her bra and let the girls out before she changed her mind.

The grin fell off Kyle's face. He made a strangled sound in the back of his throat.

Her fingers went for the button on her jeans.

No turning back now.

But given the look on his face, she didn't have any interest in turning back. She wanted to take it all off for Kyle.

The question was, did he feel the same way?

2

KYLE FORGOT WHATEVER stupid crack he had been about to make about feeling green. He forgot that the paint covering him from head to toe was cold and itchy. He forgot everything.

Because Emma Gideon, his extremely businesslike and uptight coworker, had just taken off her bra, revealing a pair of perfect C-cup breasts, their tight rosy nipples winking at him. He hadn't thought she would go through with it. It didn't fit what he had seen of her personality, and he couldn't say he really blamed her for not wanting to participate. There was more to show for a chick than for him. He was just in his underwear, no big deal. Hell, he took his garbage to the curb in his boxer briefs. But given the male obsession with breasts, he could fully understand why a woman might hesitate to expose hers in a tent with a few hundred people.

But he was oh so glad Emma had, because she had just given him fodder for a thousand fantasies. Not to mention it had answered the pressing question that had plagued him at work for the past several weeks: Was that perfect shape created by a push-up bra or was it all Emma?

It was Emma. No doubt about it.

The bra had just been a boulder holder, not the creator of the magnificent cleavage she tried to cover up with thin sweaters.

Aware that he was beyond the acceptable span of time for not speaking, he forced himself to tear his eyes off her breasts, concentrating on her hand, where the red bra she had discarded dangled perilously from her thumb. He couldn't quite bring himself to look up into her eyes, knowing she would recognize the jackrabbit lust written all over his face.

"So you're going for it," he forced himself to say, hopefully cheerfully. "Cool. It will be fun." God, he sounded like an idiot. But he was getting desperate because her fingers were now undoing the snap on her jeans, and he was standing only in his skivvies. Green paint may cover up a freckle, but it couldn't do a damn thing to mask a giant boner.

He should look away. He really should look away. But that zipper was moving down now, inch by glorious inch, and he was drawn to it like a fly to honey. Really sexy honey. He couldn't look away. Not when Emma was the only woman at the paper who had never shown an ounce of interest in him. Had never shown an ounce of interest in men or sex, period.

This could be his only chance to ever see what delights she was hiding, and while he wrestled with his conscience, at the same time he wanted desperately to catch a tiny glimpse of her forbidden fruit. A scrap of white lace was bared to him and he instantly changed his mind. Time to look away. There would be no hiding his reaction if he saw any more skin, or gave himself any more time to contemplate the soft folds hidden behind that semisheer lace, or thought about the various parts of him that could sink into that very soft, moist part of her.

He looked up, but got halted en route to her face at her chest when she started to peel down her jeans and her breasts bounced from the effort. Jesus. He was trying, damn it. But it was like laying a feast in front of a starving man. His mouth actually watered. As for the fears of tenting his briefs? They were most definitely realized. He had an erection the size of the Sears Tower.

Then Emma bent over, which put her face in close proximity to that erection, and she shoved her pants past her luscious hips. He was not going to think about what could be happening in this same position under different circumstances. Kyle went to shove his hands into his pockets to prevent himself from touching her, only to remember he had no pockets.

Emma made a small sound of distress as she lost her balance trying to withdraw her foot from her jeans, and Kyle reached out and grabbed her so she didn't fall in a heap of denim and bouncing breasts. Though he would have enjoyed the view. But he wasn't sick enough to want her injured so he could have middle school fantasies.

"Thanks," she breathed, glancing up at him, her amber-colored eyes hooded. He couldn't read her expression.

Emma stood and clutched her jeans to her chest, covering her breasts. The pants, shirt, bra and plastic bag covered the majority of her bare skin. The majority of the good parts, anyway. Kyle was simultaneously relieved and disappointed.

"Here, stand in front of me until you get sprayed. I'll block you from view," he told her, because it was clear she wasn't comfortable with her nudity. Her cheeks were pink and she had inched closer to him, farther from the room at large.

If she was going to go through with this, he wanted to help her. He wanted her to trust him. And now that he thought about it, he didn't particularly want just any guy in the room to have the same view he'd had of her breasts.

Her eyes narrowed. "What's the catch?"

He held his hands up. "None, I promise. I'm just trying to be a nice guy. So sue me." He was being a friggin' Boy Scout here, with his eyes trained on her face, and she was sure he had an angle? He was insulted.

"I'm just making sure I'm not about to become a punch line."

"What kind of a-hole do you take me for?" Kyle moved around behind her and glowered at a guy he suspected of checking out Emma's butt in her—dear God—bikini panties. It wasn't a G-string. It covered her cheeks, but not much else. And those were some perfectly curved, smooth ass cheeks. No wonder the guy was staring. Kyle swallowed hard and crossed his green arms over each other, knowing his shoulders and hips were broad enough to block a good portion of Emma. He'd played hockey in high school and he'd kept up with his weight training. There were no skinny jeans in his future and he wasn't afraid to play the muscle if need be.

The guy immediately stopped his ogling. Kyle

thought so, the sick bastard. Of course he wasn't sure he was much better, as was confirmed by Emma.

"I don't think you're an a-hole. But I do think you're the office flirt and quite the prankster," Emma said, her voice dry. He couldn't see her since he was behind her and facing away, but he could hear the plastic bag rattling as she stuffed her clothes into it.

Sometimes Emma sounded like she had fallen out of the forties. "Prankster?" Kyle snorted. "Flirt? Why, because I like to enjoy myself at work?"

"Oh, you definitely enjoy yourself when you're sidling up to Gina in accounting and her cleavage. Usually when you're an hour late on your deadline."

Kyle was actually shocked. He now understood exactly why it seemed that Emma didn't like him. It was because she didn't like him.

Which was fine. Not great, but fine. She was entitled to not like him, even if he was harboring a serious case of lust for her. But she had no right to insult his professional integrity. "I've never been late on a deadline. And for your information, I have never noticed Gina's cleavage. Her husband is a good friend of mine, so Gina and I are friends. That's all there is to it."

"Never late? Are you kidding me? And are you seriously trying to claim you don't flirt with every woman in the office?"

"Never late. Not once," he insisted. He and Claire had worked out a deal where he started at eight-thirty instead of eight Monday through Thursday and then on Fridays he came in an hour early and left an hour later. Maybe that had created a perception of tardiness, but he wasn't sure why he had to explain that to her.

He added, "I'm friendly. I like people. Since when is

that a crime?" It was actually the main reason he loved his job. He got to interact with both people in the office and out in the field. It was an industry of meetings, social gatherings, sporting events and fund-raisers. He covered them all, and enjoyed all of it. He may have lost his spot covering sports over a little press-pass snafu, but in the end he had given a longtime buddy who had cancer a once-in-a-lifetime shot at meeting the Cleveland Browns football players, and so he couldn't regret his demotion.

If anything, writing his arts and entertainment column had opened up a whole new part of the city to him. And he was doing a damn good job, thank you very much. None of that seemed to matter to Emma, though.

It bugged the crap out of him that she made it sound like he was on the verge of violating sexual harassment laws. "And I don't flirt with *you,*" he pointed out.

Her gasp of outrage indicated that wasn't perhaps the best argument he could have used. The woman standing in front of him, who had originally been in line behind Emma, gave him a look confirming this. She shook her head slightly in what was clearly a friendly warning.

"Because I respect you," he added. Usually that response could get a guy out of a veritable ton of trouble. It was akin to whitewashing graffiti in his experience.

"You're a douche bag," Emma said succinctly. "Respect that."

So Emma definitely wasn't like other women. While most ladies he knew thought he was charming, Emma read it as bullshit. That was something he wasn't sure how to fix. Nor was he sure why he cared, but for some reason he did. For months it had been bothering him that Emma hadn't warmed to him, and now it felt like a twofold mission—to force her to appreciate his good qualities and to determine why she thought work and fun had to be mutually exclusive.

"Maybe I don't flirt with you because you're mean to me," he told her mildly, figuring arguing back was a tactic that wouldn't work with Emma. It would just give her an excuse to stomp away from him indignantly. If he were calm, maybe it would calm her down.

She snorted. "I am not mean to you." Weighted plastic hit him in the back. "Hold my bag," she demanded.

Kyle figured that was an invitation to turn around. So he did.

And was so glad he did.

Emma was fairly quivering with outrage from their conversation, goose bumps all over her skin, her eyes wide and snappish. The bag she was shoving at him no longer covered her breasts. They jiggled from her movements, free from their bra. Yes, he was looking. Yes, he felt zero guilt for looking. He just took the bag and waited with great interest as she stood, arms out, to receive her coating of green paint.

"You look ridiculous," she told him, jumping with a shriek as the first spray of cool paint hit her.

"You don't look so elegant yourself," he told her. Only she didn't look ridiculous. She looked delicious. Bouncy and juicy and flushed. Even her annoyance was hot. He liked to think that passion would translate to the bedroom, that when she let her cool mask of professionalism slip, she would tear a man up. She would be bossy and demanding, pushing him down while she drew his cock into her mouth…

"Why are you wearing your hat?" she asked him.

"Huh?" Kyle wished more than anything he could adjust his underwear. Things were really starting to become painful down there. All this up and down. It wasn't good for a guy. "Because my keys are under it. I'm not sure I trust this whole numbering system." He'd left his wallet and phone in the car, but he didn't want his keys getting mixed up with someone else's.

"You can't wear that in the shoot." The woman who was spraying Emma, a heavily tattooed girl in her twenties, gave him a look of disapproval. "Ian doesn't allow any props."

"I know. I'll take it off before it's time to shoot."

"You're wearing your keys on your head?" Emma asked him, stepping forward as the handler deemed her fully painted. "You look really silly."

She was walking like Frankenstein, wet arms out in front of her, knees locked, her face shiny and very, very green. Some of the paint had strayed into her hair so that she looked like she'd been caught in an angry game of paintball and lost. Her nipples could have passed for a couple of undersize Brussels sprouts given their color, and she had scratched her nose, so the flesh peeked through the paint. Just for the record, he wasn't the only one looking silly.

"If you call me a silly goose I'm going to make fun of you. Just a warning," Kyle said.

She stuck her tongue out at him, a pink moist thrust through her green lips. It shouldn't have been sexy, yet somehow it was. He couldn't help but imagine that tongue on various parts of his body, sliding along, flickering over his flesh to torture him.

Kyle shifted uncomfortably. He needed to get away from her before the story here became him pushing her against the nearest wall and entwining his green body with hers in some sort of alien porno.

Fortunately, he was saved from potentially enormous embarrassment by a man speaking into a microphone. "All participants, you need to start moving into the warehouse where volunteers will show you to your spots."

So they started shuffling forward, dozens of people in shades of green ranging from moss to emerald, and others in variations of brown. Emma hesitated. Kyle leaned forward and murmured to her, wanting to reassure and relax her. "Has anyone ever told you that you look good in green?"

Emma snorted. "No. It's not on my color wheel."

"Maybe they never saw you in head-to-toe green. Because it's working on you right now."

"Uh-huh."

When she was directed to a spot against the wall of the warehouse with a cracked window above her head, Kyle said, "Work it, girl. Make love to the camera."

Her lips twitched, like she was actually considering laughing. He took it as a good sign.

"Hat off!" A burly woman with a do-rag on her head and a clipboard in her hand snarled at him.

Kyle stripped off his hat, dumped his keys into it and thrust it behind his back as he moved into position beside Emma. He let the hat drop to the ground, his keys making a reassuring clinking sound. They had a way out of this place, that's all he cared about. After the shoot he planned to interview some participants, but for the most part, he had all the necessary facts from the press release the artist's team had released to the *Journal*. An opinion column was his favorite kind.

"How are you doing?" he asked Emma.

Her hip was bumping into his. "I don't feel like art. I feel like a big naked emerald idiot. Do you even see the photographer?"

"No." All he saw was a bunch of green butt cheeks as the people in front of them were instructed to lie on the floor on their stomachs. "I'm glad we get to stand. This building is probably radioactive. I don't want my junk touching the ground even wearing briefs." He shifted uncomfortably at the thought. "I would like kids one day."

What had once been a thriving steel mill was now a crumbling warehouse with broken windows, the concrete beneath their feet reduced to a siltlike dust. Now that he thought about it, he wasn't crazy about being barefoot. There was no way in hell he would lie down on the floor and breathe that rubble in.

"I thought they made steel here before it closed. How dangerous could that be?"

Kyle pointed to the sign hanging at an awkward angle. "That dangerous."

It said Days Without An Accident: 3.

"Oh. Well, all the machinery is gone. And they said the shoot wouldn't run that long."

Great. Now she was reassuring him. He was supposed to be the man here, easing her nervousness about her nudity. Instead she was snaking her hand over and slipping it into his and squeezing. Wait. Nothing wrong with that.

Kyle squeezed back.

"I'm sure your virility is intact," she told him.

There was no doubt about that. Kyle let his thigh

brush hers, and their shoulders bumped. He glanced over at her. "Promise?"

She gave a short laugh before snapping her lips shut. "Yes."

"You didn't even look." He was playing in dangerous territory here, but he was a gambling man. He would bet she wasn't going to slap him in the middle of the photo shoot.

Emma turned to him, her tongue moistening her lips nervously. "Kyle…what are you doing?"

"Flirting with you."

"Why?"

"Because you're attractive. Which I've always known, but today has given me a whole new appreciation for that fact."

"You are not attracted to me."

"Um, my Jolly Green Giant says otherwise." He didn't mean to brag, but anyone looking below his waist would see his erection. There was no disguising it, boxer briefs or not.

"Your…" Her eyes dropped. And widened. "Oh. Oh."

He wasn't sure he'd ever heard Emma speechless before. It was satisfying, to say the least.

She was still staring at his jock.

All the attention had it jumping a little. Which made her jerk away like she'd been stung by a bee.

Kyle smiled. He loved his job.

3

EMMA KNEW SHE was staring at the tent Kyle's penis was making. Jolly Green Giant, indeed.

She was holding his hand. And she had the overwhelming urge to tangle her body up with his on a big bed. Neither of those things made sense.

She also knew she was naked except for a tiny pair of underwear, so she couldn't explain her odd reaction to him other than the obvious—she was trained to equate nudity with sexy times. That was the only explanation for why her nipples were suddenly as hard as the steel that had once been shipped in and out of this warehouse. Why her insides were molten and her fingers itched to reach out and give his erection a hard squeeze to see his reaction.

It couldn't possibly have anything to do with Kyle himself.

Which she knew was a total lie. She'd been attracted to him since the day she'd met him two years ago, when he had been led around the office by Claire and introduced to the drooling staff. Even the men liked him—they saw Kyle as a man's man, a golf buddy.

But none of them were standing here covered in body paint, bare leg squashed against his, staring at his erection.

"Emma." His voice was tight, pained.

She dragged her eyes off his briefs and forced them upward. "Yes?" she asked breathlessly.

"Do you think—"

But whatever he'd been about to say was drowned out by the sound of the man with the megaphone, yelling for their attention.

"Okay, I need everyone to stand still in the positions you've been given. Ladies along the back wall, I need your arms up to form the letter "I" in front of your chest, got it?"

"That's you," Kyle murmured.

Emma moved her arms automatically, feeling a little stunned. Why did she have the feeling that Kyle had been about to ask her out? Why would he do that? He wouldn't. He wasn't attracted to her. Or at least that's what she had always thought until today. But he clearly was attracted to her, as was evidenced by what she had seen hiding beneath the green.

That didn't mean, however, that he would ask her out, so why had she jumped to that conclusion?

Because she wanted that conclusion.

Ugh.

It was a relief to cover her green breasts. Not that anyone would have been able to see much of anything, given that she was one of two hundred people and she was slathered in paint, but it still made her feel better. She would no longer be on display for Kyle or for future internet trawlers.

"Mr. Bainbridge wants to thank all of you for participating. He'll only need to shoot for a few minutes, and when you all see the results, I think you'll be pleased to see how he has captured the sense of people being reduced to the walls of a crumbling manufacturing economy."

The words jolted her out of her musings about Kyle and back to the real business at hand. Was that an official statement? Emma repeated the words back in her head, wondering if she could quote that in her article. But unless this guy was the photographer's spokesman, she had to tread lightly.

"There's the man of the hour," Kyle muttered. "It's about freaking time. My paint is starting to crust and flake."

"Where?" But the words were barely out of her mouth when she finally saw the photographer, Ian Bainbridge, as he climbed onto a platform set up on the other side of the warehouse. His camera and equipment were already there, ready to use immediately. Emma had of course researched the artist. She knew he was originally from New Zealand, and that he looked like a former soccer player who had gotten in touch with his emotions. He wore a lot of black rocker T-shirts with blazers and tweed bowler hats. He also had funky black glasses that appeared in some photos of him and not in others. Today no glasses and no blazer adorned him, but a hat jauntily perched on his head as he made adjustments to his camera.

There was also very clearly a bodyguard behind him, which was no surprise given that the attention of his stalker had escalated in recent months, as reported by the Pittsburgh paper where Ian had shot the month before. Emma wondered what sort of desperation drove someone to follow another human being around and pretend you were in an actual relationship with him. Fantasizing about Justin Timberlake at age twelve was normal, but creating chaos at his concert was not. And this had the makings of a celebrity-crush stalking.

The shoot itself lasted all of ten minutes, if even. It seemed like Ian pushed a few buttons, then he was climbing back down off the platform. Emma felt a little let down, frankly. You stripped to your undies and were dolled up as an alien—you expected the occasion to feel momentous. Instead, she just had a cramp in her calf from the position she had been standing in, and her nose itched. She was already lamenting the loss of the panties she was wearing, even if they were plain white from the discount store. They were comfy, with strings that didn't dig into her hips. Now she had to toss them.

Plus there was clearly no way in hell she was going to be able to get anywhere near Ian. He disappeared behind a bevy of handlers. There was no one who looked like a stalker, either, whatever a lovesick crazy was supposed to look like.

"Someone thinks he's a rock star," Kyle said with an eye roll, pulling off the wall and moving his arms back and forth. "Man, I'm stiff. That took forever."

"It was ten minutes."

Kyle bent over and scooped up his hat and keys. "Ten minutes I'll never get back. I don't know. I mean, I dig photography, but this all seems a little…melodramatic. And I'm still not sure why we're green."

Emma kind of agreed, but she wasn't about to admit it. "Who are we to say what is art and what isn't? And ten minutes ago you were saying the exact same thing." She joined the line that was forming to reenter the tent and collect their belongings. The other attendees were chattering all around them, an air of excitement buzzing about the cold warehouse. It was June, and yet despite the season and the dozens of warm bodies, there was a definite bite in the air. "I'm cold."

"I noticed." He eyed her chest.

"What?" Emma looked down at her taut nipples and flushed. "Seriously?"

"I can't help it! You're not wearing a bra. It's bullshit if anyone thinks men and women can take off their clothes and not be tempted to look at what everyone has got. It's human nature. I call bullcrap on these shoots. I think Bainbridge is just a perv who wants to see naked bodies."

Emma wasn't sure if Kyle was joking or not. "This seems like an extreme way to go about it. The internet is full of images of naked people." But she did agree with him that it was hard not to be curious in the face of mass nudity. Which was why she was more than ready to put her shirt back on. She did not relish standing around in line with a crowd. At that very second, as she averted her eyes from an older gentleman's droopy derriere, someone could be looking at her behind and coming to the same droopy conclusion. It wasn't natural. Inevitably, it was bound to bring out the middle school in at least a few people. Like her. Kyle wasn't really doing any better.

"You were the one who said you were looking forward to stripping in public," she reminded him.

"I know. Which just proves my point—men and women should not be naked in groups together."

"You're contradicting yourself! You told me this

wasn't an orgy." It didn't feel like an orgy. It felt cold and itchy.

"It isn't. But it seems like it should be. Like this is just a way to skirt the issue."

Emma sighed. "I can't think about it anymore. It's stressful. I just want my bra back."

"Hey! Seems like there's some sort of commotion in the tent," Kyle said, up on tiptoes to see over the heads of those in front of them.

Emma was a good six inches shorter than him and she couldn't see anything at all. The voices had gotten louder, and word started making its way down the line in an audible buzz of shock until it finally reached them.

"Some people's bags of clothing got stolen," the woman in line ahead of them said with no small amount of excitement.

"What? Stolen?" Emma automatically crossed her arms over her breasts tighter. "What do you mean?"

"Some nut stole everyone's clothes."

Her clothes were gone?

Emma felt like she was going to faint.

KYLE GAVE A short laugh, amused because it seemed so obvious. Why wouldn't someone steal clothes? It was the perfect prank. As a "prankster" himself, according to Emma, he should know. "Holy shit. That figures."

But when he saw Emma's face, he cut off his laughter. She looked like she'd had a piano dropped on her foot. "It's okay. I have my keys, remember? We can at least get out of here."

"Naked! We'll have to leave naked!" She squeezed her arms tighter across her chest, like that was going to alter the facts. "This is awful! How does something like this happen? What good does security do if someone can just—" she waved her arms around madly "—steal your clothes!"

"Emma, it's okay," Kyle said, hoping he sounded reassuring. She was clearly starting to panic and people were looking at her, including one guy in his sixties who leered at her chest. "I'm sure I have something in the car you can cover up with, and hey, we don't even know that our clothes are missing. What are the odds?"

But the odds were not in their favor. It figured. As organizers bustled around trying to sort out the situation and quickly process people whose possessions were intact, it became clear that they were two of about forty people whose bags had disappeared. Kyle felt more than a little annoyed now that he had confirmation it was their stuff, and now that he had time to think about it. Those were eighty-dollar jeans in that bag, plus his favorite blue T-shirt, which chicks said brought out the blue in his eyes.

It was kind of like when the airline lost your luggage or the dry cleaner stained your favorite dress shirt. But those were accidents that all fell under the umbrella of Shit Happens.

This was a nutter intentionally trying to ruin their day. Or rather, Ian Bainbridge's day. So if Kyle wanted to look on the bright side, this would make his column that much more interesting. Not to mention, he begrudgingly supposed, this would be an entertaining story to tell for years to come. He might even find it funny, later, when he'd showered and his eyelids weren't crusty with paint.

A couple of people were furious, shouting at the volunteer staff, but most just grumbled and wrote down their information for the organizers. The police were called, but Kyle had no intention of sticking around until they showed up. Emma had been ogled enough for one day. He had the sneaking suspicion that if he didn't get her home soon, she was going to have a meltdown of epic proportions. For a woman wound tighter than a top, she was holding it together remarkably well, but he suspected she had just about reached her limit, given the way she was bouncing on the heels of her feet and tearing the flesh off her lower lip with her teeth.

"I can't believe this!" she exclaimed for about the tenth time.

"I'm actually surprised it's never happened before," Kyle said truthfully as they exited the tent and headed to his car. "I mean, it doesn't seem like it would be that hard, and it's definitely disruptive, which was clearly the goal here." He gestured back to the distraught crowd still in the tent.

"It's ridiculous," she snapped. "Who does something like that? It's just…childish."

"It's actually criminal. I wonder if they have any chance at all of catching them. Presumably it's the same woman who caused trouble at the other shoots, but it's not like there are security cameras anywhere around here anymore. This steel plant is a ghost town." Kyle picked his way carefully across the old parking lot, watching where he walked. "Careful, there are all kinds of glass and gravel lying around." He looked at Emma's bare feet. "Do you want me to carry you?"

"You're barefoot, too," she pointed out. "And you don't need me crushing you deeper into the pavement."

"My feet are callused. I won't feel it. But yours look

delicate." They did. Emma had her toenails painted red, and her feet were smooth and unblemished. They were filthy from the warehouse, but he could tell she got frequent pedicures, and she was clearly no athlete. Emma screamed workaholic. Given the lushness of her curves, he liked to imagine her lounging around on a chaise pinup-girl style in her spare minutes, instead of attacking a ball in an adult soccer league. But what did he know? Maybe she made flag football her bitch on Saturdays.

"I don't really think anything about me is particularly delicate," she said. "But I do love a good pedicure."

Kyle imagined her soft foot sliding down his leg. Bending down, he cleared his throat and presented his back to her.

"Hop on." Now that the image of her lounging on a sofa in her garter belt had popped into his head, Kyle really wanted her to lounge on him.

"I'm only wearing underwear, Kyle. There is no way I'm hopping on your back. Come Monday, we do have to work together in an office setting."

As far as he was concerned, Monday didn't exist. There was only today, and a parking lot full of broken glass. "We're not in the office right now, and you seriously should not be walking in this." He sincerely did not want her to get hurt, but he had to admit, he also wouldn't mind her legs wrapped around his waist.

"It's fine." She indignantly took a step forward and immediately winced. "Ow. Damn it, I just stepped on a rusty nail." Using his arm for leverage, she leaned down and inspected her foot. "Good thing I've had a tetanus shot. Gross."

Kyle fought the urge to roll his eyes. "I offered you a solution." He couldn't help but point that out again.

She made a face at him. "These are my choices? Step on a rusty nail or wrap my painted legs around you while I'm topless?"

Kyle grinned. "Doesn't sound like a hard choice to me."

Emma flushed. "You know what I mean. I'm no Skinny Minnie, by the way. Are you sure this is a good idea?"

He couldn't prevent himself from glancing at her breasts again. She had all the right stuff in all the right places, as far as he was concerned. "I think you're perfect. And don't insult my manhood. I can carry a woman."

"I think we've discussed your manhood enough already today." Emma glanced around at the other people who were picking their way across the parking lot. No one was paying the slightest bit of attention to the two of them, despite their lack of street clothes. "Okay, fine. But we're never going to mention this again. Ever. I don't want to hear any cracks about it today or any day hereafter. Got it?"

"Got it." Later, he would wonder why the thought of her hopping onto his back had him so excited. Right now he just wanted to enjoy it. "Well, if a piggyback ride makes you uncomfortable, I'll just pick you up."

He did just that, before Emma could change her mind. Leaning over, he scooped her up into his arms while she gave a squeal of shock.

"Kyle!"

"Yes?" Oh, man, he was in heaven. Or maybe he was in hell. Because the feeling of Emma in his arms was so amazing and yet, he wasn't going to be able to do anything about it. Or was he? Emma seemed to be warming up to him. Maybe with a little more effort, and the right circumstances, he could find himself feeling more of the delicious curves he'd been treated to all day. He bounced her a little to adjust her in his arms, her skin against his, her breasts perilously close to his own chest, her hands reaching up automatically to entwine around his neck to stabilize herself.

"Nothing," she said, eyes wide, green lips parted in an expression of shock.

Kyle gazed at her briefly, well aware of how enticing the curve of her backside was as it bumped against his waist. Her mouth was close enough to his that he could simply lean forward and kiss her. Would that fall under the same rules as him carrying her? If he kissed her, would she allow it as long as he didn't mention it on Monday? Or would she yank away and end up crashing to the ground?

Better not chance it.

He made his way to the car without incident, though he couldn't say he exactly enjoyed walking barefoot across ancient gravel. He was starting to feel like he was back in college. This whole scenario was remarkably similar to a frat party where he'd gone Jell-O diving with a date and had wound up handcuffed to a chain-link fence.

Hmm. He could hope for a better ending here.

Setting Emma down, he retrieved his keys and beeped open the passenger door.

"Thanks for driving me home," she said as she climbed in.

"No problem. I probably have something you can,

you know, cover up with." Kyle looked in the backseat. Nothing but an old fast-food bag. The trunk revealed a tire iron and a length of rope. Uh, not quite what he had in mind. Finally, he came back around and bent over in front of her.

"What are you doing?" she squawked.

Not what he'd like to be doing, frankly.

"Maybe there is something in here." After popping open the glove box, Kyle stood up triumphantly with a handful of paper napkins. "Aha!"

Her lips pursed and she looked like she was debating whether to laugh or cry. "Thanks." Grabbing them from him, she unfurled one and stuck it over her left breast. The right got the same treatment.

Kyle suddenly wanted to laugh himself so he backed up and went around to the driver's side.

"I'm sorry about your upholstery," she said, trying to put the remaining napkins under her butt.

"Don't worry about it. It couldn't be helped." Kyle was fascinated by the way she was lifting her backside up, her napkin-covered breasts jutting out.

"Wait a minute," she said suddenly. "I can't go back to my place! I don't have my key!"

Oh, this day kept getting more and more interesting.

"No worries," Kyle said. Really, it was like fate was handing him a Golden Ticket. With Emma forced into his company, surely she would see the merits of exploring the chemistry that had been sizzling between them all day. "You can come to my place."

Where they would have a little green on green action if he had anything to say about it.

4

EMMA LOOKED OVER at Kyle, horrified. She had no house key. She didn't keep a spare key outside her apartment because everyone knew that was the fastest way to get robbed. She had been on the police-blotter beat for six months and it had convinced her that a key under the welcome mat was a safety risk akin to jumping rope with a live power wire.

Her next-door neighbor, Mr. Stein, had her spare key, but he was eighty-six years old and there was no way in hell she could ring his doorbell like this, painted green, with fast-food napkins stuck to her boobs. The man would die of a heart attack and she could not have that on her conscience. The only choice she really had was to go with Kyle and borrow a T-shirt and some basketball shorts.

Lord help her.

Shifting on the seat, hoping she wasn't smearing paint onto the upholstery, she bit her lip. "Can I take a shower at your place? This paint is actually start-ing to pull on my skin." As it had dried, it had tightened, and she had to admit, she was about done with the whole thing.

Maybe once showered and clothed, she would be much less aware of Kyle and her own reaction to him. She crossed her legs tightly, wishing the deep ache between her thighs would ease up. Unfortunately, she suspected there was only one way to make it go away, and down that path lay disaster.

Or ecstasy.

Emma shook her head, irritated with herself. No. She could not. Would not. Ever. With Kyle. Not while they still worked together. She'd seen the results of fraternization between coworkers too often to be insane enough to fall into the same trap. There had been Jenny in Copy, who had slept with the head of Advertising after the holiday party and had been so embarrassed by her drunken enthusiasm that she'd quit. Bill and Stacey in their online department, who had been hot and heavy for two months, had broken up and wound up shooting staples at each other in their small shared office space. Dating, sex, love and relationships all made people emotional and irrational. It didn't mix with work.

Though one could argue she and Kyle didn't technically work together. They just overlapped in the same office space. Which was a lame rationalization and she knew it. It would be hard to sit in a meeting with ten people if one of them had seen you naked.

But Kyle had basically already seen her naked. She was almost naked right now.

Emma dug her fingernails into her emerald knees. Why did it seem like all her reasoning was evaporating into thin air and they hadn't even gotten to Kyle's yet?

She reminded herself that Claire would never be okay with an in-office affair between two staff writers. And if anyone would pay the price for it, it would most likely be her, since Claire was fond of Kyle. As in, Claire wanted to bang him herself, Emma was fairly certain.

"Sure, of course you can take a shower. And I'm sure I have something you can wear home." Kyle pulled out of the parking lot. "Man, I'm starving. I want to go through the drive-thru, but that's probably not a good idea."

"No." Emma shook her head vehemently. "Definitely not a good idea. They have cameras, you know."

Kyle laughed. "That would really get people at McDonald's talking, huh? Good thing we don't have that far to go. I live downtown."

It was a good thing, Emma realized, as they cruised to a stop at a red light. She glanced to her right and was met with the startled gaze of an older woman in the car next to them, her hands gripping the steering wheel. Before she opened her mouth to comment to Kyle that they were already getting people talking, the woman whipped out her cell phone and snapped a picture of Emma.

Horrified, Emma simultaneously slouched down in her seat and yelled at the woman. "Hey! You can't do that! Delete that! Delete!"

Realizing the woman probably couldn't hear her, she hit the button for the window to glide down and pointed, gesturing to the phone and making frantic throat-cutting motions in what she hoped was the universal language for "get rid of that shit."

"What's the matter?" Kyle asked.

"She took my picture!" Emma felt the heat of mortification flushing her green cheeks. The woman was resolutely looking in the other direction, clearly having no intention of deleting anything.

"No one will recognize you. And she couldn't have gotten anything from the neck down."

"Somebody could recognize me!" As the light turned green and Kyle started driving, Emma flipped the visor down and angled it so she could see herself in the mirror. What she saw had her gasping in horror. My God, it was worse than she'd thought. "I look…insane," she said, feeling faint.

Her hair was shot out in all directions, the paint acting as a holding gel, her face the bright emerald green of the rest of her body, with the whites of her eyes and her teeth gleaming in stark contrast. The napkins tufted up from her chest. "I look like a frog eating barbecue!"

Kyle started laughing so hard he ended up coughing. After a second, Emma flipped the mirror shut and felt the corners of her mouth turning up. Maybe it was a little funny. Besides, his laughter was infectious. He laughed with zero restraint, deep from his gut. Emma couldn't even remember the last time she had laughed like that.

"It's not funny!" she protested, even as she started giggling. He was right. No one would ever recognize her. That was a definite positive.

"Oh, yes, it is," he managed to say between chuckles. "I've never heard anyone describe themselves in quite that way, and the hilarious thing is, it's true."

"Oh, it is, is it?" Emma exclaimed, unable to deny the ridiculousness of the situation. "Thanks a lot!" She peeled one of the napkins off her breast, balled it up and threw it at him.

It bounced off his green chest. He just laughed harder, but he did give a token "ow."

"Be quiet. There is no way that hurt."

Kyle glanced at her and his eyes bugged out. With a finger he reached over and pointed, stopping a few inches short of touching her. "You left some napkin behind."

Emma glanced down and couldn't hold in a sharp burst of laughter. It just got better and better. Now she had a piece of napkin stuck to her nipple. "Are we there yet?" she asked, because really, what else was there to say?

Kyle grinned at her. "As a matter of fact, yes. We're pulling into my building now."

"Thank you, baby Jesus." Before any other Sunday drivers decided to immortalize her on the internet.

Kyle lived in an old warehouse that had clearly been turned into chichi apartments. Normally Emma would have loved a leisurely stroll around the building to admire its brick-and-iron architecture, but today she just wanted to get behind a closed door without anyone else seeing her.

That was too much to ask for, though. Almost immediately when they stepped out of the car, they encountered a man who was potentially homeless, given his layers of crusty denim and flannel, despite the warm June day. He pushed a shopping cart. Emma figured her hair was on par with this guy's, which was matted and uneven. Trying not to make eye contact, she crossed her arms over her chest and let Kyle usher her toward the door.

The shopping cart's squeaky wheels quieted as the cart slowed down, the man probably gawking at the picture they made.

"Damn hippies," they heard him grumble.

As the heavy fire door to the building closed behind them, Emma let out a laugh. "Oh, my God, he just called us hippies! What hippies do you know who look like this?"

"I don't know any hippies." Kyle shook his head. "I think they're actually extinct. But you're right, I can't imagine they would look like alien extras from a B-budget film. Let's take the stairs so we don't run into anyone on the elevator. That could be awkward."

"Very." Emma shuddered at the thought, her breast napkin flapping as she walked.

Kyle's apartment was on the second floor, so they were inside and free from any potential encounters in a matter of a few steps. Emma let out the breath she hadn't realized she'd been holding.

"What a day," Kyle said, tossing his baseball hat onto the console table in the entry.

"No kidding." Emma stood just inside the doorway, eyes sweeping quickly around the room, feeling hugely self-conscious again. For some reason, she had expected Kyle's place to be a glorified dorm room. Messy, with mismatched furniture and beer cans lying around. It was nothing remotely resembling her vision.

Kyle's place was neat as a pin, his granite kitchen counter bare of all clutter except for a coffeemaker. His couch was streamlined and modern, with one throw blanket on the arm, folded to perfection. The loft-style windows gave huge amounts of light to the space, and Emma glanced down, aware of her dirty feet on his pristine floors. There wasn't a speck of dust or dirt anywhere, and she felt the need to walk with paper towels wrapped around her unfortunate feet.

"Nice place."

"Thanks. I like it. I can walk to work." He moved into the room. "Bathroom's this way. Come on, I'll get you a towel."

"Thanks." Emma followed behind Kyle, her eyes focused on his tight butt and his firm thighs. He was very muscular, but not in a bodybuilder way. Just athletic. Natural. Her fingers itched to reach out and squeeze all that muscle in front of her. Not paying attention to anything other than his ass, Emma didn't realize he had stopped walking until she plowed into him, her hands brushing across the back of his thighs.

"Oh! Sorry." Emma jumped back a foot as she realized he had stopped to open a linen closet, and was pulling out towels.

Kyle turned, his eyes dark and unreadable. "I'm really good at keeping secrets, you know."

Her heart rate kicked up a notch and her nipples firmed, goose bumps rushing over her skin. "Oh, yeah? I imagine that's helpful in journalism. The whole Deep Throat thing."

God, did she really just say *deep throat* to him? Emma felt her cheeks burn, but hoped the paint camouflaged her embarrassment.

Kyle shook his head. "Emma, you're killing me. You know that, right?"

"No. I had no idea." Which was a lie. She was very much aware of the sexual tension running between them. They were mostly naked, standing inches apart. She had accidentally touched his thighs and his mouth was close enough that with one short lean she could be kissing him.

"You are. And I most definitely can keep a secret, so if anything else happens here today, you can be sure it will never be mentioned at the office. Or ever, for that matter, if that's what you want."

"What could happen?" Because she was a girl who liked things to be spelled out. She knew what he meant, but she needed to hear confirmation that the man she'd been attracted to for quite some time was equally attracted to her, and was offering her an afternoon delight.

"This." Kyle closed the gap between them, the towels he was holding crushing against her chest, his hand coming up to cup the back of her head.

Emma didn't hesitate, but let her eyes flutter shut as his mouth covered hers in a deep, tantalizing kiss. Yowza. It was as perfect as she could have imagined. Kyle's lips teased hers with just the right amount of pressure and finesse, his touch confident and smooth but not arrogant. There was something very soft and worshipful about his kiss, and she sighed as he pulled back.

Kyle had surprised her.

EMMA HAD SURPRISED HIM. For some reason, Kyle had expected Emma to kiss with precision and efficiency, like her office persona, or with a bold passion. He hadn't anticipated she would be so vulnerable, so feminine, so sweet. She had kissed him back, but she had let him lead, and he found that immensely appealing. She tasted like…willingness.

"So you're going to keep that a secret?" she asked,

the tip of her tongue running along the bottom lip he
had just tasted.

The message was loud and clear—Emma was ready
to play. Kyle wouldn't have guessed it of her. But then
again, he hadn't pictured they would wind up in his
apartment in the state they were in. If their clothes
hadn't been stolen, he imagined he would have just
gone home and showered solo. Whereas now he had a
shot at showering with her.

Kyle gave a silent thanks to the thief.

"That's just the beginning of what I intend to keep
secret."

Her eyes widened and her nose twitched. He had
noticed she did that when she was nervous, or considering a response. He found it adorable. Not normally
a word he used to describe women he wanted to take
to bed, but in Emma's case, it was very much true. She
was stinking cute.

"Maybe this is why you've never flirted with me,"
she said. "I can't think of a single appropriate come-
back."

"I never flirted with you because I thought you
would rip my balls off." And because he'd thought
she would shut him down so hard it would hurt. Hey, he
could admit it. "And just say whatever you're thinking."

"I'm thinking that I want to see what you look like
without the green. Naked."

Yeah, baby. "Good, because I was thinking the same
thing about you." He gave her hand a squeeze, then
took the towels to the bathroom. "You can shower first.
Unless you want me to join you?" Hey, you never knew
unless you asked.

"Uh, I don't think so." She snagged a towel from

his hand and held it up in front of her before pulling the one remaining napkin off her chest and tossing it in his wastebasket.

Two steps forward, one step back. Kyle was willing to be patient. For the next ten minutes or so. Then he was going to get another kiss, plus a little more if he had anything to say about it. There was no real reason for him to go into the bathroom with her, but he did, under the guise of turning on the shower and showing her his extensive collection of body gels.

"Here's a loofah thingie so you can scrub the paint off."

Emma took it, but she was staring at his shower doubtfully. "This is going to make such a mess. God, I hope it doesn't stain the marble. Who puts marble in a shower?"

"It won't stain." He hoped. But it wasn't like they had much choice. They were green and that wasn't going to change until they showered. He winked at her. "Have fun in there."

There was something about the way she was looking at him, her lips parted, her breasts heaving behind the towel, her toes curling on his cork floor. If he wasn't mistaken, she did not want him to leave, but she wasn't going to say that. She was waiting. For him to do it. Be the one who crossed all those boundaries and said to hell with office relations.

Well, they weren't in the office and he wanted to relate to her on a whole new level. If she wanted him to make the move, be the bad guy in a way, he was more than willing to do just that. Because at the moment all he cared about was getting inside a nice hot shower and then getting inside her.

So Kyle took back the loofah he had handed her. She gave it up easily, her breath a sharp intake of air as he moved in close to her, his hand going to the small of her back. This time when he kissed her, he deftly stroked his tongue in between her lips to mate with hers, a hot rush of lust flooding over him, encouraging him that this was definitely the right move to make. When he yanked the towel out of her hands and dropped it to the floor, she didn't protest. She let him move his body in alongside hers, the first brush of her nipples against his bare chest causing him to groan.

"I want to feel your real skin," he told her. "I want to taste you. Let me get in the shower with you." He was dipping down into the back of her panties, getting a brief feel of her bare flesh where there was no paint, her smooth ass cheek a perfect fit for his hand. He tossed the loofah into the open shower door so he would have two hands to squeeze, to bump her body into his, to make her aware of his fully engorged erection.

Her soft moan indicated she was very much aware of it, as did the fact that she was kissing him deeper and with more urgency.

"Okay," she murmured.

Kyle paused in kissing her, hands still on her back. "Really?" He hadn't thought she would agree, but now that she had, he realized it was stupid to question it. Better to just hustle her into the shower.

Before she could respond or change her mind, Kyle stepped back a foot and stripped out of his briefs, tossing them toward the wastebasket.

Her eyes widened. "Oh, my God."

At first he thought she was impressed with his stature, because hey, he was no gherkin. But then her lip started to twitch and he realized she was trying not to laugh.

"What the hell is so funny?"

"Your skin is just so white where there's no paint… and then your erection…" She giggled, her hand indicating something jutting out.

It was a good thing he had a healthy ego or this very well could have damaged him for life. But Kyle had a sense of humor, and glancing down, there was no denying it was an interesting picture. "I imagine the back looks even more ridiculous. Turn around and pull down your panties and let me see your bare ass."

"No!" She laughed and took a step backward. "There is no way. In fact, I'm getting in the shower like this."

Which she did. Panties and all, the spray hitting her body, sending green rivulets immediately to the floor of the shower. She sighed in pleasure. "It feels amazing."

"You're going to ruin your panties showering in them," he teased her. "You should really take them off." But he was okay with her leaving them on for now. It wouldn't be long before she'd be out of them, anyway. He could ease her into full nudity.

Not a problem.

"Ha-ha." She put her face directly under the spray and scrubbed at it with her bare hands.

"I don't think it's going to come off that easily. You need a washcloth." Kyle grabbed a pair of them and stepped into the shower, closing the glass door behind him. Despite the fact that water was running off her in a green deluge, the paint wasn't really leaving her body. The first thing he did was to take one cloth and scrub his face hard, feeling grateful to get the paint off his lips and eyelashes. He wanted to taste her lips, her body, in a natural state.

She shifted a little forward when he moved in behind her, angling her body slightly away from his. Her nervousness was clear and Kyle wanted her to relax. So he squirted a blob of shower gel onto one of the cloths and moved it to Emma's shoulder, rubbing gently.

His touch caused her to jump and give a little squawk. "What are you doing?"

"Getting this paint off you. You can't reach your shoulders and back to scrub them." If he were matter-of-fact, maybe she wouldn't balk. Plus, he was basically massaging her shoulders at the same time, and he could feel some of the tension immediately leaving her body.

"I have to admit, that does feel good." She sighed.

Turning slightly to the right so she wouldn't get poked in the ass with his throbbing erection, Kyle continued to put pressure on her shoulders, working his way down her back. The water was bouncing off him, steam rising, tendrils of her hair starting to curl in the heat. The smell of the gel and her skin as it was reclaimed from the paint was intoxicating, and Kyle was feeling languid and aroused, in no particular hurry to reach his destination because he was definitely enjoying the sensual journey.

Though that feeling was tested a little when she reached forward and braced her hands on the marble wall in front of her. Kyle's body tensed at the gorgeous vision she made, back arched, legs slightly apart. He wanted to kick her feet farther apart because it was the perfect position to enter her from behind. The idea took hold and he had a hard time shaking it. To distract himself, he kissed the shoulder that was now squeaky-clean and free of paint in front of him.

Then he went for the shampoo. "Here, let me wash your hair for you."

"No!" she immediately protested. "That's creepy."

"Creepy?" Kyle laughed. "Emma, I think you have a funny way of looking at things." Actually, he was starting to think she had intimacy issues, but he wasn't about to say that out loud. She'd stomp off in a snit, and hell, who could blame her? He didn't exactly want his character flaws pointed out to him, either. Especially not when he was naked.

"Well, it is," she insisted. "It's too parent-child."

Way to make him feel gross. Talk about a mood killer. He let his erection nudge her, his hands snaking around her chest to brush over her nipples. "Honey, nothing we're doing here is even in the same hemisphere as parent-child, so we're just going to forget you ever even said that. I mean, think about it. When the stylist at the salon shampoos you, does it feel like your mother doing it?"

"No," she admitted. "Not at all."

He nibbled on the back of her ear, enjoying her sharp intake of breath. "Then let's leave your mother out of this altogether. Because I've never met her, but I think it's safe to say I wouldn't want to do this to her."

Kyle turned her around and gave her a searing kiss before going down on his knees and peeling off her panties despite her exclamation of shock.

Parent-child his ass. He was going to make her forget she even had parents.

5

KYLE WAS STRIPPING her panties off her. He was going down on his knees, and she strongly suspected he wasn't down there to pick up the errant loofah. Emma reminded herself to breathe. Then she reminded herself to stop reminding herself of things and for once in her freaking life to just close her eyes and enjoy something.

It was easier than she would have thought. After the initial shock and knee-jerk awkwardness of realizing she was very naked, her most intimate hills and valleys bared to Kyle, she relaxed, her hands on his shoulders for balance. First he lifted one foot and then the other to divest her of the paint-plastered panties. His hand slid back up her leg as his mouth pressed a kiss on the slope where her hip and thigh met.

Okay, she wasn't going to lie. That felt good. His touch was sensual, slow, not greedy, his tongue starting an erotic path right in the direction of her clitoris. If he had tossed her against a wall and dived in, she probably wouldn't have enjoyed herself. She needed a guide during sex, not a hit-and-run driver. A good host, that was what she needed. Someone who anticipated her every need and who confidently directed conversation.

Kyle was definitely doing all the talking, his tongue having completed his journey to land on her clitoris just briefly, so achingly short of a swipe that Emma moaned in protest when he moved it lower immediately.

"What's the matter?" he murmured.

"Nothing," she said, because she wasn't going to ask him to suck her clit. She wouldn't. She couldn't. It would feel too weak of her. The water ran over his back in a green river, exposing his bare flesh, and Emma drank in the sight of him between her legs. On his knees. For her. Steam rose around them, and she suddenly felt like she was in the tropics, under a waterfall with the man of her dreams. What was actually happening was frankly almost as implausible. She was receiving oral sex from Kyle, the office hottie. How crazy was that?

Insane, that's what it was. As insane as the way he was making her feel as his tongue stroked casually over her inner folds, as if he had all the time in the world, as if he could eat her all day and most of the night. It was the biggest turn-on, that he was just gripping her thighs and making a meal out of her like he wanted nothing else quite as much. She dug her fingers into his flesh a little deeper, her body responding to his ministrations by growing moister, her inner muscles tightening, her nipples becoming painfully tight peaks.

It usually took substantial effort on a man's part to bring her to orgasm because she didn't have the ability to let go. She knew that was her problem, had tried to coach herself to relax, breath deeply, but more often than not she had been unsuccessful, and she and her partner had wound up frustrated. But with Kyle, she forgot she was supposed to let go. She just did it.

Instead of the tension she normally felt, the deep in the shoulders, clenched thighs and teeth sensation when a man was pleasuring her, or attempting to pleasure her, Emma felt relaxed. Her muscles were like melting chocolate, soft and pliable, and she sagged against the shower wall, brushing her hair back out of her face.

"Oh, yes," she said, not even sure why she said it, because she didn't talk during sex. It just wasn't something she did, because she was usually concentrating so hard on finding an orgasm that she didn't have time for words. But they just floated out with Kyle, making her sound like someone completely different than herself. Emma moved her hands from his shoulders to his hair, playing with the short strands, enjoying the tactile sensation of touching him while he did such delicious things to her. She heard her moans growing louder, but she didn't care. This was moanworthy. Kyle was doing things with his tongue that had to be illegal in at least twelve states.

When her orgasm began, it didn't hit her with a slap the way it usually did. Instead it began gently and swelled, big, juicy and intense waves of ecstasy rolling over her for longer than she could have imagined possible. When it came to a slow stop, she blinked the water out of her eyes and stared at Kyle's head, stunned. That was hands down the best oral-sex orgasm she'd ever had. It had been easy, full, long.

Maybe it was the hot shower water. That must have contributed to her relaxation. Or maybe Kyle had a tantric tongue. She decided she wasn't going to worry about it. She would savor it for the moment, and later on, possibly dream about it.

"Mmm," Kyle said, kissing her inner thigh. "I enjoyed that. I hope you did, too."

Duh. "Yes." It had been amazing. She opened her mouth, wanting to say something more, something appreciative, but the words stuck in her throat. God, she was terrible at this. It was no wonder she was a workaholic. Her social skills sucked.

Feeling tension popping up in her shoulders, her teeth digging into her bottom lip, Emma watched Kyle stand. His chest was still streaked with green, but his face was mostly clean, his large hand rubbing over it to swipe away the water, and if she wasn't mistaken, some of her. He gave her a slow, naughty smile, making the ache deep in her belly begin to burn anew. Moving close to her, he gripped her hips and kissed her hard, the taste of her still on his tongue. As he kissed her, erasing the tension she'd been manufacturing, he eased her back into the corner of the shower.

Then lifted her left leg so her foot rested on the ledge.

"What are you doing?" she asked, feeling breathless and overheated.

It became obvious what he was doing when his fingers stroked inside her sensitive body, clearly open for him from the position he'd moved her leg into.

"I'm making sure you're ready for me." He nuzzled her neck, running his lips over the tight bud of her nipple, all while his fingers quickly found a rhythm that had her grabbing the wall for purchase. "You are."

"Oh, yeah, I am," she agreed, nodding. She wanted to experience his penis firsthand now.

Instead, he shifted away. That was not going to work. "Where are you going?" she demanded.

KYLE APPRECIATED THE tone of voice Emma used. She sounded completely irritated with him, and he grinned, knowing she wanted him inside her almost as much as he did. "Don't worry, sweetheart, I'm just taking care of things."

He had condoms in the drawer, and if he leaned, he could reach them. It was a stretch, but he didn't want to get out of the shower and leave her, so he kept one hand on her hip and with the other reached all the way into the drawer and snagged a foil packet. Water shot all over the floor with the shower door open, but he figured that's what towels were for. Within sixty seconds, he had the condom on and was back where he had started, only Emma had dropped her knee down, covering her from his view. He wasn't having any of that.

But another thought occurred to him. "Are you comfortable? Do you want to move to the bed?" He didn't want to be an inconsiderate lover. Frankly, he wanted to be the best lover she'd ever had.

"I'm fine. Just please…before I die." Emma's face was an arousing mix of desire and agonized anticipation.

Kyle felt his mouth flood with hot saliva. There was something so vulnerable about her, the way she seemed more overwhelmed by her needs than in control of them. It made him feel like she had entrusted him with something big—her satisfaction. He knew she wasn't the kind of woman who was going to ask for anything, yet she was asking him to bring her to completion, to slake her desire, and he wanted to do that more than just about anything. His own need was secondary.

So he kissed her, a deep press of his lips over hers, while he gently urged her knee back up with his hand. With his thumb, he found her clitoris and massaged it, enjoying the way her breath caught on a sigh of pleasure. When he moved in between her thighs and teased his cock at her warm entrance, he shifted his hand upward so that he could play with her nipple. Easing in slightly, he closed his eyes at the hot feeling of her surrounding him, but he forced himself to pull back out, causing them both to involuntarily groan.

"Kyle," she murmured, and he wasn't sure he'd ever heard his name spoken quite that way.

He pushed back in. "Yes?"

"Never mind."

Before he fully penetrated her, he was back out.

"Kyle!"

"Yes?"

His eyes were half-closed, the water hitting him in the shoulder and bouncing off his thigh. Her hair was damp, her skin dewy and pink. Steam rose around her as she occupied the corner of the shower. It was surreal, unbelievable, yet at the same time Kyle felt completely in the moment.

Knowing what she wanted, knowing his own control was shattering with each teasing stroke, he pushed inside her again, all the way, filling her completely with a ragged groan of ecstasy. She felt like perfection. He moved slowly, easing in and out in a steady rhythm, not wanting to give in to the frantic urge to pump at her jackrabbit-style. Slow and smooth was better, and he was rewarded with her body swelling around him, and her startled moans as an orgasm rocked her.

That's what he was talking about. It was different than her earlier one. Or maybe it was just he was aware of it from a different perspective. But it seemed bigger, more powerful, everything tight, her fingers digging into his arms. Kyle figured there was no reason to delay his own gratification, and it felt so damn good to have her shattering beneath him that he braced his left hand on the shower wall and exploded inside her.

When they both quieted down, Kyle leaned his forehead on Emma's and sucked in some air. His throat hurt from groaning. His thighs were cramped from the position he had been in, and he was suddenly aware he had no feeling in his toes because they were curled over the shower mat to brace himself. Water dribbled in his mouth, water that had gone lukewarm. He peeled himself off Emma and gave her a grin.

"This has been a very relaxing shower," he told her, pulling off the condom so he could rinse himself.

"*Relaxing* isn't exactly the word I would use for it," she said, lifting her light hair off her cheek. It fell with a wet slap on her shoulders.

"Oh, no? What would you call it?" Kyle bent over and pumped his hand full of shower gel from the bottle on the ledge and started scrubbing himself below the waist, working away the last of the green paint and their lovemaking.

Emma's eyes weren't on his, but were watching his hands moving around his junk. Finally, she looked up and gave him a sardonic half smile. "Wet. That's what I would call it."

He laughed. "Literal. I like it."

"We are journalists, after all."

She bent over to pick up a washcloth that had dropped to the floor, giving him a heart-stopping view of her ass. Five more minutes and he would have grabbed on and taken her from behind, but he needed some recovery time. Plus food. He suddenly remembered he was starving. He was willing to forget that for a little while longer so he could enjoy the view of her naked flesh as long as possible. There was something amazingly erotic about watching Emma soap up her bare breasts, hands cupping them, the last of the paint disappearing under her ministrations and the force of the spray.

The best part was Kyle didn't think she had any idea how freaking sexy she was. She was just being Emma—efficient and matter-of-fact. But that made it even more arousing, because it was like he was being given a peep show into her personal shower. Unfortunately, he gawked so heavily, his own hands no longer moving, that she suddenly became aware of him and shot him a look that could only be described as suspicious.

"What?"

He shook his head, enjoying her discomfiture. She amused him. "Nothing. I'm simply enjoying the view."

She gave him a pursed-lip look of disapproval. "The view is going to be leaving because this water's getting cold."

He supposed he should be pleased that Emma had let her guard down as long as she had. Hell, if anyone had told him yesterday he'd be doing her in the shower he'd have laughed his ass off, but now that he had seen her relax and open up—literally—to him, he wanted to see more of that side. Instead, she was retreating into the prim-nanny mode she usually subjected him to.

So he gave her backside a light slap as she opened the shower door and stepped onto the bath mat.

"Hey!" She jumped, then shot him a glare.

"You missed a spot," he told her blithely.

But she just rolled her eyes. "Does that work with women? I mean, seriously? The Matthew McConaughey act?"

He should be insulted, but he suspected Emma was secretly enjoying herself. If she wasn't, she would have left, right? So she could bristle and act unimpressed all she wanted, as long as she did it with her pants off.

At the same time, though, he wasn't stupid enough to let her know he was onto her exaggerating act. He would need to play a delicate game if he was going to get Emma to agree to a round two. He was fairly certain if she didn't, he would throw a tantrum.

"It always works with ordinary women," he told her, following her out of the shower with a grin. "But you're special."

It was a gamble, going for the blatant sarcasm. If she was more insecure than he realized, she might be offended. But Emma snorted, the corner of her lip turning up.

"And you're a tool."

He shrugged. "I've been called worse."

Emma was vigorously drying herself off.

"Why don't you leave a layer of skin on?" he suggested calmly, choosing intentionally to dry his hair off first with a towel so he was standing in front of her buck naked.

She tight-rolled the towel she was holding around

herself, so she was covered from armpit to knee. He was about to mention that something was wrong with this picture, when she did something that absolutely shocked him to his core. In the best friggin' way possible.

Emma came right up behind him and slid her hands down his back and over his ass, gripping him tightly. "I have to admit, I've been thinking about doing that all day."

Damn. He wished he had known that. He wished he could see her face right now as she greedily touched his backside, but he was going to take what he could get. The getting was pretty good, he had to admit. The uptight Emma Gideon had shagged him in the shower and was now feeling up his butt. This was a day for the history books.

"I'm glad you decided to take action," he told her.

"I figured if none of this can be mentioned come Monday, then I might as well take full advantage."

"That's very practical of you," he said, sucking in a breath when her fingers brushed over his hips, almost reaching his suddenly eager-all-over-again cock.

"I'm a practical girl," she said. "Some see it as a flaw."

"I have to tell you that I very much appreciate it. I mean, practically speaking, I'm sure you'll agree we should get our fill of each other today since tomorrow we have to pretend it never happened." Kyle placed his hand over hers and drew it a little closer to his budding erection.

"The idea has logic to it." She moved in front of him and let her hand stroke over him. "But I thought you said you were hungry."

"I'll just eat you," he said, and bit her shoulder to back up his point. "Nom, nom."

EMMA LAUGHED. She couldn't help it. There was a reason everyone thought he was charming. There was just something easy and infectious about him. Post-sex, she had panicked for a moment, the need to flee strong. It was the effect of spending a lifetime listening to a conscience that dictated toeing the line and never taking risks. That voice reared up to tell her she'd made an enormous mistake, one that couldn't be undone. She had broken the golden rule of Thou Shalt Not Bang Your Coworker. Lord knew her grandfather had made it clear many times that her mother's giving in to grand passion had altered the course of her life, and not for the better.

But then Emma had thought about it, and frankly, she'd be stupid to walk away from this day without enjoying it to the fullest. She wasn't eighteen, and she and Kyle had already discussed the outcome of this like mature adults. Which meant she could have more penis, guilt-free. Because that had been the Best. Sex. Ever. Imagine what else they could do given a bed.

Which meant she was going to have to feed him more than her inner thighs if she wanted him to keep up with the pace she was planning to set. She may not be the most successful at relationships, but she did understand men, and they couldn't concentrate when they were hungry. It was a fact.

So she dropped her hand and stepped back from him. "We can order Chinese."

"Can we fool around while we're waiting for it to be delivered?"

"Yes." That was a good compromise, and honestly, she could use a little fooling around in her life.

"Then I'm good with that." Still gloriously naked, he strode into his bedroom across the hallway and opened his dresser drawer. "Do you want boxers or briefs?"

Emma followed him, intimidated all over again with how neat and tidy he was. "You can wear whatever underwear you want." It wasn't like she was his girlfriend. It wasn't like she was his anything. Her cheeks flushed. Why had the thought of meaning nothing to him, and pretending that none of this had happened, suddenly upset her so much?

Because she was lame. That was her only conclusion.

"No, I meant do you want to wear my boxers or my briefs? Or do you just want a pair of jeans or something and you can go commando?"

"I am definitely not wearing your briefs." Because she would be forced to stick a sword in her gut and die if they didn't fit her. She had hips and a booty. "I'll just go commando. Do you have sweats or something?"

Five minutes later, Emma was guessing that Kyle would rethink wanting to fool around with her. She wore sweats cuffed at the ankle because they were a foot too long. They were super long in the crotch, too, yet they clung to her backside. He'd given her a T-shirt with the Ohio State mascot, Brutus Buckeye, on it. One of her nipples pushed through his nutty grin, which was awkward.

This was not her best look. But then again, Kyle had kissed her when she'd been green, so maybe she shouldn't worry about it. Maybe she shouldn't worry about anything. It would be a novel experience for her.

When they went into his living room, he pulled his tablet off the kitchen counter and flopped down next to her on the couch. "What kind of Chinese do you like? I like it spicy."

"I like it as plain as possible. Steamed rice, steamed vegetables."

"Gross. I guess we won't be sharing." He hit a few keys and found a delivery place.

"I need to spend some time outlining my article," she told him. "And we should follow up with the cops and see one, if they have our clothes, and two, if they have any leads on who stole them."

He shot her a look. "I thought we were going to fool around."

Emma felt defensive, even though she was being irrational. The truth was, spontaneous didn't stick with her. She was already back to feeling like there was no way Kyle could be attracted to her, the spice-hating workaholic wearing his ill-fitting sweats. Once those thoughts seeped in, it wasn't a huge leap to stressing out over her article and her career in general, which made her want to work.

"What? It has to be done. We can fool around, too. Later. When it's finished." There was a window of opportunity here to take her article in a direction that wasn't a vanilla reporting of an ordinary seminude photo shoot, and she didn't want it to close on her. It annoyed her all over again that he never seemed to have a care in the world, and that she could never achieve the same state of relaxation.

"It can wait twenty minutes. We'll mess around, we'll eat. Then we can work. I promise." His fingers were flying over his iPad. "Order sent. It will be here in thirty minutes. Now let's get busy."

"Writing the article?" she asked, hopefully. It was going to stress her out if she didn't knock this piece off, even though she knew she was behaving like a workaholic. What did an hour matter? It wouldn't kill her to have some fun. So why did it feel so painful?

Because she was lame. That seemed to be the conclusion here yet again. There was a pattern here. She'd freaked out undressing at the shoot, she'd freaked out about sleeping with Kyle, and now she was freaking out over an article she knew she could write in forty-five minutes even if she had the flu. So why couldn't she just relax? It was a rhetorical question.

"No," he told her.

"I have a confession to make," she blurted out. "I know you think I'm insane, that I'm a workaholic, but the thing is, my dad left when I was two and my mom worked really hard to raise me. She worked as a bank teller during the day and on weekends she cleaned houses. I would go with her. I saw the way people talked to her—like she wasn't worthy of their time. She's an amazing person. She's generous and funny and she can cook like those guys on Top Chef. So I work hard because I want to be able to make her life financially easier, to help her out and repay her for all she sacrificed to raise me. And because I don't ever want someone to talk to me the way they did to her." Emma took a deep breath and blinked at Kyle, her heart racing after her verbal vomit.

Maybe that had been oversharing.

She wasn't even sure why she would share something so personal, other than the fact Kyle had helped her through the photo shoot, reassuring her, taking a negative situation and giving it a positive spin. She appreciated seeing that different side of him, and she wanted him to know there was more to her than met the eye, as well. She was the sum total of her parts, and until the shower, he had only seen two of them. Now she wanted him to see a third.

Again to his credit, Kyle didn't bat an eye at her speech. He just said, "I get it. But I have the opposite approach to life. My dad died of a heart attack at forty-three and my brothers and I barely even knew him because he worked so much. Even when he was around, he was stressed about money, stressed about his job selling insurance. He died alone in a hotel room at a conference in Chicago, and I decided no matter what I did as a career, I was always going to make sure I enjoyed my life and wasn't living to work. I work to live."

Emma blanched. "Oh, God, Kyle, I'm so sorry about your dad. How old were you?"

"Fifteen. And it sucked. My mom was left with three teenaged boys to raise, and my older brother ended up dropping out of college and coming home. So maybe I'm not as aggressive as I could be at work, but the truth is, I love the job, and I'm fairly good at it. Will I be a star reporter for the *Wall Street Journal?* No. Because I'm not willing to sacrifice everything and I'm okay with that."

"Sure." Emma rubbed the palms of her hands on his borrowed sweatpants. "I guess that is something I've never really asked myself. Am I willing to sacrifice everything for success?" But the answer was there already—she didn't have time for friends, time for fun, time for exercise. The charity she felt so strongly about, which funded job training for impoverished women and single mothers, never got her time anymore, only a check each month. Plus she couldn't remember the last time she'd seen her mother. It had to be at least three weeks ago and they only lived twenty minutes apart.

A hot, sick feeling rose in her mouth.

"I'm not criticizing you, you know," he told her. "My point is just that neither way is right or wrong, but we're shaped by our own experiences. Ours resulted in opposite approaches to our careers. But the bottom line is, if you're happy, that's all that counts, Emma."

"Who the hell said I was happy?" she exclaimed. "I'm not even remotely happy! Before today I hadn't had sex in over a year. That is not happy."

Kyle stared at her for a second, then he burst out laughing. "You crack me up. So why don't you relax a little and carve out more of a social life for yourself?"

She shrugged. "Because my mom is so proud of me. She lives vicariously through my success and I want her to see I've done well. To see that everything she gave up was worth it."

"If she's like my mom, my guess is she just wants you to be happy."

It was all so simple and obvious that Emma felt a little sheepish. "Yeah, you're probably right. Maybe I do need to chill a bit with the work hours. There's no reason I can't have some fun, too."

His eyebrows went up and down. "I can help you in that pursuit."

Oh, she had no doubt he could. "Are we back to the fooling-around-before-dinner request?"

"No, of course not. Unless you want to. Or we could continue talking. Talking works." His expression grew serious. "I know I joke around a lot, but I'm glad you shared your feelings with me, Emma. I appreciate the trust you've put in me."

She felt her throat close up a little. It was starting to occur to her that maybe Kyle had more depth than she'd ever given him credit for, and he was certainly being a nice guy. "I appreciate you listening. And you gave me some great, nonjudgmental advice. I do need a better balance between work and fun." Then because she had gone about as deep into her feelings as she was comfortable with, she gave him a saucy smile. "So you think you can help me with that? I'd like to see some proof."

No hesitation on Kyle's part whatsoever. He flipped down the waistband of his basketball shorts and sprang his erection free. "Big fun right here."

Oh, my. Did he just sit around half-hard all the time? It boggled the mind.

She suspected he thought she would scoff or say something prudish. That he expected her to shut him down and say his gesture was more tease than anything else, despite her attempt at bringing the conversation back to fooling around. Because she had a pattern of resisting fun. But deep inside she had a naughty girl. She just usually locked her up in a dark closet where she couldn't come out. But she was going to open that door and let her out to play for a few minutes, and hopefully catch Kyle completely off guard.

So she said casually, "That does look like fun."

Then she bent over him and covered the length of him with her mouth.

"Emma." He gave a growling gasp of shock. "Holy shit."

It was the kind of reaction she never got, and she really, really enjoyed it. Slowly drawing him in and out of her mouth, Emma listened with fascination as the timbre of his voice changed, getting more ragged and deeper with each little groan he gave. She felt powerful, excited, in charge. Aroused.

She could sense he was about to orgasm right when a knock came at the door of his apartment. She paused.

Kyle cursed. "Are you kidding me? He couldn't get here two minutes from now?"

"I guess I should stop." Emma started to sit up.

Shaking his head, Kyle gripped her shoulders. "Absolutely not. I'll just call him back in five minutes and then tip him really well. He'll be barely down the block when he has to turn around."

Emma was astonished. That would have never occurred to her. She just didn't think like that. It seemed so against the rules. But for some reason, the urgency, the knowledge that the deliveryman was standing on the other side of the door, stirred up her competitive nature. She wanted to finish what she'd started, so she applied herself to the task with renewed vigor.

"Damn," Kyle murmured. "Sweetheart, you have mad skills."

Emma wouldn't have thought it would be possible to be so pleased at a sexual compliment, but as he exploded, she felt a sly satisfaction she never had before.

"You're welcome," she said as she sat up, wiping her lips and grinning at him. "Now go recover our dinner."

He saluted. "Yes, ma'am." He leaped up with an excessive amount of energy, tucking himself away, then cracking his knuckles. "Damn, girl. That was hot. Smokin' hot!"

His enthusiasm made her laugh. A giddiness swept over her. She couldn't remember ever really being proud of herself in bed before.

Following him to the door, she watched him sprinting off after the deliveryman, who had just started down the stairs, cell phone to ear, probably calling his boss to report the problem.

"Hey, man, wait up!" Kyle was yelling. "Sorry, you caught us at a bad time, if you know what I mean."

Apparently the guy did know, because even though Emma could no longer hear what they were saying to each other, they did a fist bump. Then the deliveryman glanced down the hall at her and waved. He gave Kyle a grin. Sheepish, Emma waved back and retreated back into the apartment.

She was certainly experiencing a lot of firsts today. Group partial nudity, being called a hippie, sex with a coworker, scandalizing men who brought her steamed rice.

But none of this existed tomorrow, so she wasn't going to sweat it.

She was just going to enjoy it.

6

KYLE WAS ON a bit of an orgasm-and-spicy-chicken high and he couldn't help but smile at Emma as she carefully ate her steamed broccoli and boring brown rice on the couch next to him. He felt that as they'd spent the day together, he had been inadvertently peeling back the layers of her personality. And had made some shocking discoveries. There was the hardworking, efficient, broccoli-eating, workaholic Emma that he saw every day. Then there had been the vulnerable Emma, the one who had hesitated to take her top off at the photo shoot, and who had waited for him to take the initiative in their lovemaking. Then there was the naughty Emma, the one who shot him a sassy look before going down on him. He wanted to see how often he could get that Emma to emerge from behind her mask of disapproval.

"So what do you like to do in your free time?" he asked her, picking up their earlier thread of conversation about the lack of fun in her life.

"What free time?" She gave him a rueful look. "I don't know. I grocery shop. Clean. Take in my dry cleaning. Squeeze in a workout when I can."

"So no, like, secret ballroom-dancing obsession or golf weekends?"

"No."

"Wild nights drinking shots of tequila?" He would pay money to see Emma do a shot of tequila. Though he was sure she never would. Drinking shots meant losing control and that wasn't her style.

"Hardly."

"So there isn't anything that you used to like to do that you miss?" Kyle knew he might be pushing it, but he felt compelled to at least make her understand that balance in life was important. She'd admitted she wasn't happy. One thing he could say for certain was that he was. He loved his life and the people in it, and he was grateful for his job and his free time.

"Well…" She looked at him over her chopsticks, hesitant.

"What?" he encouraged.

"I used to love to go sing karaoke in college."

Now that surprised him. Karaoke required an ability to not give a shit what anyone else thought and he hadn't imagined she would feel that way. "Really? That's awesome." It was. He had a sudden image of Emma making love to the microphone while singing Carly Simon. "What was your specialty?"

"'Like a Virgin' by Madonna."

Kyle choked on his noodle. "What? For real?"

"Yes," she said sadly. "I used to crawl around on stage and everything. It was fun."

The idea of Emma crawling on the floor seductively had his shorts feeling tight. Damn. Which gave him an idea. "We should go, then. Tonight. You can brush up on your Madonna and we'll have a blast."

"No!" She looked horrified at the thought. "It's been years. I only sing in the shower now."

He raised an eyebrow. "That you do."

Her cheeks turned pink. "That's not what I meant. My voice is rusty."

"So? No one can sing their way out of a paper bag at karaoke. That's half the fun. Showmanship is what counts, and I would say crawling on the floor would do that."

"We have this story to work on. Plus I'm not dressed to go anywhere."

Kyle eyed the T-shirt he'd given her to wear. She was straining the limits of Brutus Buckeye's face with her breasts. No, he couldn't say he really wanted her going out in public like that. He'd already had enough of strange men eyeballing her breasts for one day. She needed a bra, stat, if they were going out.

"Okay, let's do this. We'll work on the article for an hour or so, swing by your place for your key and a change of clothes, and then we'll go to karaoke for an hour or two. I'll have you in bed by ten. And by in bed, I mean naked with me between your legs. Sound good?"

Emma stared at him in astonishment. Her mouth opened and closed twice. But then she finally just said, "Okay."

Surprised at how easy that had been, Kyle pulled his iPad across the table. "Excellent. Let's see where they have karaoke on Sundays. Then let's knock this article out."

EMMA WATCHED KYLE, head bent over his laptop, typing, his cell phone propped on his shoulder as he talked into it. The coffee table was a minefield of his electronics and half-eaten Chinese food. She had realized he was a master multitasker. He could research online, eat and interview attendees from the shoot on the phone all at the same time. At the moment, he was asking the photographer's assistant for a preview photo from the shoot. All without a shirt on.

Emma wasn't even sure how he'd gotten the assistant's number, because she sure in hell didn't have it. She was sitting on hold with the police after having been passed from department to department for ten minutes. No one seemed particularly eager to discuss the clothing theft at the shoot.

"Well, if you're not interested in giving us a photo or an interview with the photographer, I think we both know the direction this article is going to take. We're going to be left with nothing but the negative angle of the theft, and I'm sure Mr. Bainbridge doesn't want his art to be reduced to the police blotter."

Emma listened to both Kyle and the weird organ music coming from her cell phone and wondered how he got away with the tactics he did. If she said that, they would hang up on her. But then again, she didn't have the charming easiness he had. He made people feel comfortable enough to let their guard down. Hell, look what she had done today. She had slept with him and had agreed to go to karaoke. It hadn't even been that hard to talk her into, either. If you had told her yesterday she would be doing any of this, she would have scoffed.

More than scoffed. She would have snorted in derision.

But not only had she slept with him, she was discovering she actually liked Kyle as a person, and it was starting to freak her out. She felt the tightness in her chest, that ever-present anxiety she felt, easing around him. He was fun, kind, easy to be around and thoughtful. Yet he was a flirt and ultimately not her type. Hell, she wasn't his type, either. They had agreed that tomorrow none of this was going to be mentioned again, which was definitely for the best. So she needed to focus on what was happening, not what could or couldn't happen. It was so hard to live in the now, but she was trying.

She tried to remember that an hour later when Kyle was urging her to put her name in for karaoke. This had been a bad idea. She hadn't sung in public in years, and half the time in college she'd had a buzz going from cheap beer, which she had hated, but drank purely for economy. "I don't know..." she told him nervously, glancing around the bar at the motley crowd. There was everyone from twenty-one-year-old sorority girls to crusty older gentlemen wearing toupees.

"You said you had fun doing it, remember?" Kyle handed her one of the beers he had ordered, taking a sip of his own.

Oh, goody. Beer. Her least favorite drink. But she didn't imagine they had a good Pinot Grigio in this place. It was most definitely a dive, with sticky floors, an odor of stale fried foods and cigarettes somehow still lingering from before the smoking ban in 2004, and a female bartender who was well over six feet and looked like she had retired from a successful career in wrestling bears. Emma sipped her beer and grimaced. It tasted as gross as she remembered. The bartender glared at her. Yikes. Emma turned and fought the sudden urge to laugh. This was all so ridiculous.

"Fine. I'll do it." She slapped her beer down and went over to the guy operating the karaoke to put in her request. When she got back to Kyle at the bar, he was staring excitedly at his cell phone.

"Hey, look, Bainbridge's assistant sent me a picture we can use in our article. She says I have to explicitly state it is not the final product, but an unedited proof. Look at it." He turned the screen toward her. "Now I know why we were green."

Emma squinted at the tiny photo, but she realized that while the majority of the participants were shades of brown and gray, blending into the walls of the warehouse, those painted green created a giant dollar sign that seemed to undulate down into the floor of the abandoned and crumbling building. "Wow, that's actually pretty cool."

"It makes a statement, that's for sure. Where are we?" Kyle swiped his screen to make the image larger and moved it around until he found them in the photo.

When he blew it up and Emma saw it over his shoulder, they both started laughing. "That about says it all, doesn't it?" Emma said, taking another sip of her god-awful beer.

"I look stoned."

He did, she had to admit. Kyle was grinning, a sort of lopsided dopey smile, his head slightly tilted. His eyes were half-closed and he wasn't looking at the camera, but slightly to the left at Emma.

She, on the other hand, looked like she'd been electrocuted. Her eyes were enormous, her mouth open, shoulders so tense they were practically hugging her ears. The good news was that her breasts were fully covered, and she wasn't easily recognizable because of the green paint, but nonetheless, it was not a good shot of her. "I think I took the instructions not to move a little too literally. I'm as stiff as granite."

"We look like crap," Kyle said cheerfully. "Let's not use this one for our staff photos."

The idea of that was so hilarious it made Emma laugh harder. "It's worse than my eighth-grade yearbook picture. By the way, my God, could we be more total opposites? A picture says a thousand words and all that."

It was right there, in green, how different she and Kyle were. Yet they'd had a wonderful afternoon, she had to admit. He'd forced her to relax, and she had forced him to work. Hmm. It was kind of obvious who had gotten the better end of the bargain there.

Kyle was about to say something, but the DJ's voice blared over the speakers. "Emma, we have Emma up now. Put your hands together, people."

Oh, Lord. She took a few more gulps of her beer and tried to remember why she had enjoyed this. She felt nervous, but Kyle gave her a quick kiss and a thumbs-up as she made her way to the makeshift stage, which was really just plywood plunked down behind a decade-old teleprompter. She hadn't started out with "Like A Virgin" because that would be presumptuous and doomed to fail. She needed a warm-up, so she was singing "Before He Cheats" to open the pipes.

It took a few notes, but once she got past the first verse, Emma hit her stride, and definitely remembered why she had loved to sing. It was freeing. Exhilarating. It was like throwing her hands up in the air as the roller coaster plummeted down a hill. Behind the microphone she wasn't Emma, she was Carrie Underwood telling a story and it was fun. A lot of fun. The room cheered and swayed, and girls nodded their head in agreement as they listened to the lyrics about a woman beating the crap out of a cheater's truck.

"Whoo, thank you!" Emma gave a little bow at the end of the song, a bit breathless at the effort and the applause. Before she could pause to think about it, she turned to the staff and signed up for "Like A Virgin." If she was going to break out of her shell for the night, she might as well burst out of it with gusto and really do it in style.

Kyle high-fived her when she returned to him. Flushed and laughing, she drank the rest of her beer and ordered another one. Halfway into that, she found herself wedged between Kyle's legs with his hands inappropriately placed on her backside, though she had to wonder if it really was that big of a deal. He'd already touched her butt, right? And this wasn't exactly a classy establishment. Was it really so terrible if they canoodled a little? It wasn't like they were digging into each other's clothes, it was just a wandering hand that felt very, very nice.

Since none of this mattered tomorrow, why not go for it?

Feeling a little reckless, she let him kiss her with tongue, even as the bartender glowered at her in disapproval.

"That bartender hates us," she whispered in his ear.

"She's just jealous." He nibbled on her bottom lip. "She wishes she looked like you. She wishes she sounded like you. She wishes she had a hot guy kissing her."

Emma laughed. "Hot guy, huh?"

"Absolutely." He gave her that lopsided grin that was so damn sexy. "Oh, wait, you're up again."

She was. This time, Emma stepped onto the stage with confidence. She played to the crowd and after she sang the first line, extolling the virtues of being touched for the first time, she called out, "This is for you, Kyle!" Then she proceeded to sing and crawl with all the sexual aplomb she could muster, and damn if it didn't feel amazing.

KYLE COULD NOT believe his eyes or ears. Emma had an amazing voice. She was a confident singer, a strong alto, and she could wrap the crowd around her little finger with her sensual stage presence. She sauntered, she strutted, she flirted, *she winked* for God's sake. She had changed into a pair of jeans and a tight top at her place, and he had to say that when she seductively crawled on the floor, lip curled back, breasts leading the charge, he felt a lust so powerful it almost knocked him off his stool. That was before he even took in the view of her firm ass perkily encased in those skintight jeans.

"She's something else," the guy next to him said to Kyle, giving him a nudge.

"Tell me about it," Kyle murmured.

"You're a lucky man."

"That I am." He most definitely was going to get lucky again tonight. It was written all over the way Emma's eyes watched him, the way she'd given him that comical shout-out, the way she'd let him kiss her in public without once questioning if they might be seen by someone they knew.

So when she came offstage flushed with triumph, threw her arms around his neck and declared, "Let's do a duet!" he wasn't about to say no.

Which was how he found himself on the little stage twenty minutes and two beers later overdramatically crooning "Turn around bright eyes" at the appropriate moments in her version of "Total Eclipse of the Heart." He had to admit, he was having a blast. He couldn't sing for shit, but Emma could, and hers was the hard part. He was just comic relief in the background, and the more he clenched his fist and sang emphatically and soulfully to Emma, the more the crowd cheered. As her passionate pleas got stronger and she played right back to him, her eyes sparkling, voice strong and high, Kyle fell to his knees for the climax.

Emma shot him a grin before she pushed him on the shoulder and turned her back to him. The song slowed into its final sad ending. Kyle imagined in a video this would be where a wineglass crashed against a marble fireplace, but here in the dumpy bar, he settled for emphatically tossing his empty beer bottle into the trash can nearby and gazing forlornly at Emma's back.

They brought down the house. What could he say?

But when Emma turned around, laughing, the look in her eyes was so hot he knew it was time to leave.

"That was awesome!" she declared.

"It was," he agreed, pulling her by the hand over to the bar, where he nodded as people gave them congratulations and grins. "You're awesome! Let's go."

"Already? But we're having fun."

He tried to explain it to her. "Emma, I have been

watching you seduce this bar crowd for the last hour and a half. I am so turned on right now I'm going to die if I don't get to be inside you in the next twenty minutes. Literally die. Dead. Collapse from a heart attack because every drop of blood is in the biggest erection I've ever had in my life. Does that make sense to you?"

She blinked, her mouth dropping in sympathy. "Oh, dear," she said, channeling the retro Emma he found so oddly sexy. "I guess we should address the problem as soon as possible, then."

Which might explain how he found himself buried deep between Emma's thighs on the floor of the foyer of his apartment a mere ten minutes later. They hadn't made it to the bedroom. They'd barely made it out of the car. It was only by the most dedicated determination not to be a total dog that he restrained himself to only sliding a finger down into her jeans in the car while he drove, then leaping out in the parking lot before he was tempted to take her over the gearshift.

She was beneath him on the hardwood, making the most delicious sounds in the back of her throat, and looking up at him as if he were the most amazing lover she'd ever had. It was a powerful feeling, stroking inside her welcoming heat, eyes locked together, and Kyle felt an odd floating sensation he'd never experienced before, like he was completely grounded in his body, yet at the same time watching himself, watching something shift and change inside him.

He couldn't blame it on being drunk. He'd only had the two beers.

But that didn't change the fact that Emma felt amazing beneath him, the breasts he'd hastily bared bouncing as he pounded into her. She was going to have a sore back tomorrow, among other things. He should pause, move her to his room, make love to her slowly and at great length.

Emma screamed out as she had an orgasm and he abandoned the idea of pausing, or even slowing down. He allowed himself to come, shouting out the way he had been wanting to do for the past two hours, her fingers desperately digging into his back. That's what he was talking about.

When they both stared at each other, breathing hard, speechless, Kyle peeled his sweaty body off hers and helped Emma to her feet. She limply let him take her hand and lead her to his bedroom, where they collapsed on his bed.

"Holy shit," he managed.

She never said a word.

Kyle fell asleep with his hand on her breast. He dreamed of a fox with blond hair singing about his ability to make her feel touched for the very first time.

It was a deep sleep, but not necessarily a restful one.

He felt a little afraid of the fox.

7

EMMA BLINKED HER EYES for the seven thousandth time as she stared at Claire in their standard Monday-morning meeting. Her eyes felt like she'd massaged them with sandpaper. Someone had replaced her tongue with a larger one, she had a bruise on her lower back that throbbed, and she was uncomfortably aware of her sore vagina.

She was mildly hungover. But mostly she was mortified, and she was studiously ignoring Kyle seated at the end of the long boardroom table, even though he had given her a small grin that said volumes when she'd come into the room.

When she'd woken up in Kyle's bed, she had sat straight up, shocked she had spent the whole night. Shocked she had been so carried away by passion she'd had sex with Kyle twice, but never in a bed. The shower and the floor. Not to mention she had given him oral sex on his couch, with a deliveryman knocking on the door. Who did that?

Clearly, she did that. She wanted to do it again. Her mind wandered. That had been, hands down, the best sex of her life. Kyle was so muscular and so *hung*. It made her blush to think about it.

"Emma, what do you think?"

Startled, Emma jerked, hitting her knee on the table. What was she thinking? Nothing that could be said out loud. Ever. "Well."

She hadn't been listening. She never daydreamed during Monday meetings. Or any meetings. She listened attentively and took notes. But now everyone was staring at her and she'd been caught with her pants down, which about summed up her current issues. She'd had her pants down a lot the day before, and it had clearly screwed up her concentration. Mind racing, she tried to remember what had last been said, her heart pounding beneath her crisp white blouse. Panicking, she could feel her mouth growing hot.

"I'm sorry to interrupt," Kyle said, "but Emma and I discussed this in great detail yesterday and I don't think she wants to downplay the crime that took place at the photo shoot. If the photographer has a stalker, it's very possible the incident with the stolen clothes is related, and Emma wants to make that connection." He looked down the table at her. "Right?"

Grateful he had just clued her in on what they were discussing, she nodded vehemently. "Absolutely. I think the public should know the shoot was compromised despite security being present. There is a potentially dangerous, and clearly determined, stalker following this photographer. She has disrupted three of his last four shoots in some manner or another and it's always involved the volunteers. In Louisville, she masqueraded as a coordinator and sent a hundred volunteers away from the shoot, claiming it had been canceled. In

Pittsburgh, she littered the chosen area with garbage so it had to be moved at the eleventh hour. Now this? She clearly has a point to make and none of us know what it is, or if it will escalate into violence."

"I don't know." Claire frowned, her perfectly sprayed hair not moving an inch as she shook her head. It was so immobile there were times Emma wondered if it were a wig. She was waiting for the day when Claire turned her head, but her hair stayed facing front.

"It seems like a side note to me, not a full story," Claire added.

"Well, we're running two pieces on the shoot on Wednesday," Kyle pointed out. "So I don't see why Emma's can't delve into the stalker to some extent."

Wishing she had a glass of water the size of a swimming pool, Emma nodded again. Why was she letting Kyle speak for her? But it felt like her brain was moving with the speed of an anemic turtle and she couldn't formulate a proper argument. Worst of all, as she stared at Kyle, she was having a difficult time banishing from her head the image of him between her thighs, making her feel more alive than she had in months.

Not what she should be thinking about in a meeting with her coworkers. Crossing her legs in her pencil skirt, she silently cursed her libido. This was the absolute wrong time to have a sexual flare-up. She had a case to make for her investigation into the stalker and she did not need to be distracted by Kyle's hotness factor. This was why the day before was a mistake. Even if it didn't feel like a mistake, and she didn't want to give it back, it clearly was still a ginormous lapse in judgment and she was paying the price for her spontaneous bad-girl behavior.

Damn it. She needed to get it together. "I agree," she managed to say.

"If we run that," Claire said, "we'll lose all co-operation from Bainbridge's camp."

"So?" Kyle asked. "After we run these on Wednesday, we won't be dealing with him anymore, anyway. I already have the photo from his assistant and we won't need a follow-up piece."

"Unless the stalker does something at the next shoot," Emma said.

"No, we're not going to follow this one," Claire said. "Not unless something really interesting happens in the next three days. If the stalker attacks him, then we have a story."

So that was it? No story? Emma tried to cover her reaction, but she was disappointed. "I need to at least mention the clothes disappearing."

"Sure, but make it lighthearted," Claire said, fiddling with the chunky gold necklace she wore. "This is Life & Style for Chrissakes. People want humor and entertainment, not crime."

At that moment Emma knew that if she were forced to stay in Life & Style for more than another year or two, she would die of boredom. She wasn't allowed to mention crime in a negative way? Because crime was so funny. She mentally rolled her eyes.

"We'll run the picture with Kyle's story."

"What? Why?" Emma sat straight up in her chair, almost spilling the coffee of the woman, Sandy, next to her. "If my piece is the straightforward write-up of the shoot, and Kyle's is an introspective column, then mine should have the photo."

"No, we're giving it to Kyle. He was the one who

secured it, so he can run it." Claire gave Kyle a fond and flirty look. "Good boy."

Oh, gag. Emma fought the urge to throw up in her mouth. Her cheeks went hot and she breathed in and out, steadily, trying to contain her emotions, which were a mix of disappointment and anger. Claire was being intentionally biased.

"No, Emma can have the pic. It goes better with her story." Kyle straightened his tie and leaned back in his chair.

Claire's eyes narrowed. "Why are you so concerned with Emma's story today? Did you two bond over mutual nudity?"

"What? No. We weren't nude," Kyle pointed out, his fingers drumming on the table nervously.

Or maybe it just appeared nervous to Emma, who suddenly felt enormously guilty and as if everyone in the room knew what they had done. She could feel Sandy's and Claire's eyes on her, along with the three other staff members present. Kyle was looking anywhere but at her.

"I knew this was a bad idea," Claire said, eyeing Emma over her massive coffee cup, a perfect lipstick print on the side. "Neither one of you should have participated in the photo shoot. If any in-office fraternization comes out of this, heads are going to roll, do you understand me?"

"Sure." Emma nodded, her throat tight. "We're professionals, Claire." Professional what, she wasn't sure. "You don't have to be concerned." Emma would be concerned enough for all of them. Because she had already fraternized with Kyle and there was no undoing it. Nor did she particularly want to. It had been damn good fraternization.

As Emma studiously avoided looking at Kyle, Claire moved on to another subject.

But Sandy leaned closer to Emma and murmured, "What does Kyle look like with no shirt? As good as I imagine?"

Emma stared at her coworker, shocked. Sandy was in her fifties and had been married for thirty years. But she looked so eager, Emma couldn't help but nod. "Yes. Yes, he does." It was the truth.

"I knew it." Sandy sighed. "If I were ten years younger and single, I'd climb him like a tree."

Emma coughed. "Wouldn't that violate Claire's in-office fraternization policy?"

"It would be worth getting fired over."

Would it? Emma thought about the day before. The night before. Her multiple orgasms. She wouldn't give that experience up easily. But she wasn't willing to lose her job for an afternoon delight with Kyle, no matter how delightful. No one knew about yesterday, but if she and Kyle were to continue to engage in a sexual relationship, someone was bound to figure it out. Most likely Claire, who clearly had every intention of making a play for Kyle herself.

Of course she had no idea if Kyle would even want to have sex with her again.

All of it, together with her hangover, was depressing. Emma fiddled with her phone, where she'd been taking notes, and pondered how she was supposed to write a story about the photo shoot with no interviews and no information about the stalker. It was going to be two paragraphs, tops. When the meeting was dismissed, she retreated to her cubicle and stared at her computer screen, feeling tired and out of sorts. She didn't want to write the story the way Claire wanted it done, pithy and light. What was the headline supposed to read? Shenanigans at Photo Shoot?

Ugh. She was rereading her notes and desperately desiring a nap when she sensed someone behind her. Turning, she involuntarily jumped when she realized it was Kyle. "What?" she asked, more acid in her voice than she intended.

"Good morning to you, too, sunshine," he said cheerfully, like they hadn't gone to bed at 2:00 a.m. liquored up and sexed out. He leaned close to her, bending like he was checking out something on her computer screen, one hand on the back of her chair. "If you hadn't run out this morning, I would have made you coffee," he murmured.

Emma felt her cheeks bloom with color. "What happened to us never mentioning yesterday ever again? I believe that was our agreement."

"All I mentioned was that I would have made you coffee if you hadn't disappeared. I don't think that violates our agreement."

It was a loophole and he knew it, but Emma had to admit she was pleased he was making initial contact with her, and did want to talk about what had happened. It would have been a little deflating if he had truly been blank-faced, acting like not a single thing had gone down between them. That she hadn't gone down on him. "I needed to get home to change if I was going to have a prayer of making it to work on time."

"Next time," he said, finger coming up like he was pointing to a sentence on her screen.

The thought of more sex with Kyle, the realization that he desired her again, had heat blooming inside her, which both shocked and embarrassed her. She didn't get wet at 10:00 a.m. on a Monday. She just didn't, and yet every time she was near him, she was fighting arousal. "There won't be a next time. You heard Claire."

"It's really none of her business what we do outside of the office." Kyle straightened up and leaned against her desk, feet crossed, hands in the pockets of his khakis.

Emma knew that he hung around other coworkers' cubicles all the time, usually in an equally casual stance. But he was never in her office space, and she felt like it had to be glaringly obvious to everyone in the room that something had shifted in their relationship. She was certainly aware of it. Her nipples hadn't gotten hard for no reason.

"This isn't the place to talk about it," she said through clenched teeth, punctuating it with a strained smile in case anyone was looking. "But I want to point out again, you agreed that as of today yesterday wasn't going to exist."

Not that she was going to be able to stick to that directive. Nor did she really want him to, because what could be worse than a guy who would very easily have sex with you and then be okay with never doing it again? That would be awful. So she did appreciate the fact that he appeared to want to sleep with her again, but it didn't make it any less confusing. Her teeth clenched tighter and she rubbed her temple.

"Do you have a headache?" he asked. "We did put

away a few last night. I have ibuprofen in my drawer if you need some."

Was he being purposely obtuse or was he really that clueless? "I think if you leave my headache will go away," she told him pointedly, glancing around to see if anyone was watching them.

"I'll leave if you agree to go to dinner with me."

"What? Are you insane?" she asked, her voice going louder than was strictly wise. She crossed her legs firmly and wiped her sweaty palms down her pencil skirt. Did the idea of dinner and what might come after with Kyle set her ablaze like the fire of ten thousand suns? Yes. Was she stupid? No.

"I have an idea for your article," he insisted. "I think we can make something work, but we only have until tomorrow afternoon if we're going to pull it off. So meet me at my place at seven tonight. It's completely legit business." Kyle pushed off her desk and moved to leave, but on the way past her, he bent over and whispered, "Don't wear panties. You won't need them."

Emma stared at her computer, refusing to look at him as he vacated her cube. She didn't like being told what to do. She didn't want to jeopardize her job.

Yet somehow she had the sinking feeling that she wasn't going to be able to resist hearing what Kyle had to say about her story. Or his opinion on the panties she most certainly was going to wear.

KYLE WAS ABOUT 50 percent sure Emma was going to stand him up, but he went ahead and cooked dinner, anyway, and put a bottle of wine to chill in the fridge. If she didn't show, then he would eat half of the wild salmon himself and save the rest for tomorrow's lunch. The wine would keep.

But he really hoped she would be there. It meant more to him than he cared to consider.

Kyle liked women and he liked to date, but he had only been in love once, and that—a passionate affair in college with a grad student—had been doomed from the start. She had been less in love with him than in the idea of him being in love with her, and it had ended predictably with her breaking it off and him begging her to reconsider. It had been possibly the most humiliating experience of his life when he had followed her to a bar, drunk, and had pleaded with her in front of thirty people. Since then, he hadn't stayed away from serious attachments as much as they'd never presented themselves. But he had dated a fair number of women and found a lot of enjoyment in their company.

Never had he dated someone like Emma, though—someone so focused and single-minded. He wasn't sure if it was just that she presented a challenge or if it was something deeper than that, but he really did want to see her outside of the office. The day before had been eye-opening. Emma had been stern and shy and sassy at alternate times. She had been sexy and fascinating and delectable, and confident when she sang and when she sucked him. It was an intriguing combination that Kyle wanted to explore further, even as it scared him.

Besides, he really did have an idea for her story, because he agreed with the look on Emma's face in the meeting that morning that had said Claire's angle was lame. An intentional disruption of the photo shoot was not something to chuckle about, especially not when there was a prior history of contact from a stalker.

Kyle wiped down his granite countertop and stood back to survey his handiwork. He had only recently started cooking and found that he really enjoyed the creative aspect of it. He had grilled the salmon on a wood plank with asparagus and roma tomatoes, seasoned in rosemary and olive oil. A rice pilaf was resting on the stove, and he'd chosen a chardonnay to accompany it. Was he trying to impress Emma? Possibly.

But for all he knew she hated fish with a burning passion. Or she hated him with a burning passion. She hadn't exactly been all warm and fuzzy at work, but she also took Claire far more seriously than he did. He knew their boss was mostly bluster. She had no intention of firing either of them, and if they were discreet with their relationship, she would never even know.

So what if yesterday he had agreed that it would be a one-time deal? He hadn't signed a contract and really, she should at least be flattered he wanted to embark on a dating relationship with her. He couldn't say he had ever wanted to springboard a one-night stand into a relationship before, but he did with Emma.

What relationship? Kyle glanced at his cell phone. It was 7:08. She wasn't showing.

Disgusted with himself, he stabbed a piece of asparagus and popped it in his mouth. He wasn't used to feeling so off-kilter. It was annoying. He ate another spear, chewing hard. His dream about the cunning fox resurfaced and he realized he was afraid. He was scared of how quickly he was developing feelings, was scared of rejection.

The doorbell rang.

He dropped his fork with a clank and chewed faster. She'd actually shown up. He was going to get to spend more time with Emma, in and out of bed. Yesterday he wouldn't have thought that would have mattered, but today it obviously did. Hell, he'd showered and changed his shirt when he'd gotten home. Plus his bedsheets, all in wishful thinking.

He pulled open the door to his apartment after checking in the hall mirror to make sure he had no vegetable remnants on his teeth. "Hey," he said with a smile. "I'm glad you came."

Emma was glancing nervously left and right as if she expected Claire to pop up out of the fire-escape stairwell and can her. She stomped into the apartment past him, a sour look on her face. Wearing jeans and a plain white T-shirt, she spun on her heel and made a point of pulling up the waistband of her panties past her jeans to show him she was wearing them.

Kyle raised his eyebrows. "That's quite a greeting."

"I just want you to know that I'm not here for funny business."

"Good, because I wasn't planning on laughing."

She made a face and rolled her eyes. "I'm serious, Kyle. I don't want to piss off Claire."

"Claire isn't here." He moved forward, trying not to smile, knowing it would make her mad. "But you are. And I am. There's salmon in the kitchen and wine that needs to be opened. That's it. Nothing more, nothing less."

She hesitated. "You confuse me."

"Well, then, we're even, because you confuse me, too. Why are you here if you don't want to spend time with me?" Kyle stepped past her and pulled two dishes out of the cabinet and plated the salmon and vegetables.

"Because you said you had information about the stalker."

He put the plates down on his small dining table in the kitchen and went for the wine. The occasion seemed to call for it. "No, I said I have an idea about the stalker, not information. But sit down and eat and we'll talk about it."

Deftly popping the cork, he took two glasses out of the cabinet and started to pour. Emma didn't sit down. She hovered next to him so that when he turned to hand her a glass, he brushed against her. Leaping back a foot, she shook her head, holding her hand up.

"I don't want any wine."

The more she blustered, the more he was determined to get her to relax and be the Emma she had been the day before. Setting her glass down, he erased the space between them and put his hand on her curvy hip, sudden images of pounding into her warm flesh assaulting him. "Then how about a kiss?"

When she didn't run away or scream in protest, he took that as consent and brushed his lips softly over hers, letting his eyes drift closed. She did the most bizarre things to his insides. It was crazy.

"I must still be drunk from last night," she murmured.

Her hands had found their way to his waistband.

"Why do you say that?"

"Because I shouldn't be here. And I certainly shouldn't be kissing you."

"Don't worry about Claire, honestly. She's not going to fire us, and we can be discreet, right?" He hoped. He would certainly try, anyway.

"Can we?" she asked ruefully, then let go of him

and picked up the wine he'd set down. She moved to the table. "I can't believe you cooked. I'm impressed."

Yeah, those were his balls swelling with pride. "I took a class."

"You took a class?" Emma grinned at him as she sat down. "Well, bully for you, then."

"You know you sound like my grandpa," he told her, taking the other seat. "It's cute as hell."

"My mom and I lived with my grandfather when I was growing up. I think I absorbed his speech patterns. Now tell me your idea for the stalker."

"Was your grandfather as tenacious and single-minded as you?" Kyle took a bite of salmon. It was getting cold, but it was still delicious. He honestly didn't want to talk about work, but he had to or she would realize he had lured her there under false pretenses.

"Yes. I come by it honestly."

"Okay, I'll put you out of your misery, then. So here was my thought—if we can identify the stalker, then Claire will have to run the more serious angle to your story."

Emma's fork paused halfway to her mouth. "And how exactly do you propose we do that? In less than twenty-four hours the article has to land in Claire's in-box."

"Think about it. Ian Bainbridge has to know who his stalker is. If this were political, they would leave a message of some kind, you know, some sort of moral slam of his work—letters to the paper, graffiti on his exhibits. But they don't, which means this is personal." Kyle had thought about it all day, and it was the only conclusion that made sense.

"So what, like he has a sworn enemy or something?

Another photographer who's jealous? I don't have any proof, but to me it just seemed more like it was a random crazy fancying herself in love with him."

"I agree. I think that it's someone who has decided they're in love with Ian, or that he's in love with them. Maybe someone who sees the photo shoots as a betrayal of some kind. Classic stalker scenario when you're talking about a celebrity. Someone who has never met the person in question yet has decided they're connected in some way. Creepy, but it happens."

"I agree with you, but that still doesn't give us any way to figure out who this person is. The cops don't seem to have any idea."

Kyle scoffed at her naïveté. "Come on, like they've even tried. Besides, we're talking about three different cities here, so three different police departments. But I bet either Ian or someone in his camp at least has an inkling of who the stalker is, or maybe they've had communication with them. Stalkers like to send notes and leave gifts for the object of their desire."

"If Bainbridge knows who his stalker is, wouldn't he tell the police?"

"He probably has, but I doubt there's enough evidence for them to do anything about it."

Emma held up her finger. "So, one, how are we going to learn this person's identity? Two, how are we going to get evidence to prove it? Again, by tomorrow."

"I thought you were tenacious. Those are not the words of a determined journalist, which I happen to know you are."

"You're baiting me."

He laughed. "No, I'm not. I'm trying to help you, and I don't want anything in return, I swear. I just happen to agree with you that this story has legs. We just need to find them. Quickly."

"So what's our first step? Contacting Ian's assistant?"

"Done. I caught her this afternoon." Kyle gave Emma a grin. "We just happen to have an appointment to interview the photographer himself in an hour, right before he heads out of town."

That got her attention. She spoke with food in her mouth. "What? Are you kidding me? How the hell did you manage that?"

"I have my ways." Mainly being very friendly with Bainbridge's assistant, a delightful twentysomething named Rosanna. But he was not about to admit that to Emma. It would confirm all her suspicions about him. He personally didn't agree that her hard-nosed journalist approach worked in every situation. Sometimes you just needed to be nice to get the information you wanted. He didn't see it as him fooling anyone, or using her. People volunteered whatever details he was fishing for all on their own, and usually they were happy to help him.

Rosanna had been quite chatty, and though she didn't know anything about the stalker specifically, she knew her boss had a fair amount of details. She even alluded to him hiring a personal bodyguard as he had reason to believe the interest and tension surrounding the stalker was increasing.

"I don't even want to know what ways of securing information you have. They scare me. But if I could make a story out of this, that would be fantastic. There's been talk about the effectiveness of the anti-stalker laws and we could really tie this in." Her eyes were shining and her cheeks were pink, from excitement and not from the wine she'd barely touched.

"We're going to try." Kyle took a sip of his wine. "You know I used to be in Sports, obviously, and we never got a shot at doing something like this, so I understand where you're coming from, wanting to dig deeper on a serious story."

She studied him in a way that almost made him uncomfortable. She was looking beyond his words to inside of him, it seemed, and he wasn't used to that. He showed the easy, happy-go-lucky, mostly superficial side of himself to people, and for the most part they accepted him at face value and didn't delve deeper.

"Why did you leave Sports? There were rumors of misconduct, you know."

"Yeah, I know. I gave my press pass to a buddy who had caneer. He got into the locker room for the Cleveland Browns with it and got to meet the players. I got reassigned." He shrugged. "No big deal. I violated policy and I did it intentionally, so I deserved the demotion."

"Why?" she asked, clearly puzzled.

"Because the guy was dying," he told her quietly. "And he did die. It was the one thing I could give him, so I did. Regardless of the consequences. And hey, look, nothing turned out so terrible, did it? I'm on Life & Style with you, and now I'll forever be immortalized as a stoner in Ian Bainbridge's *Money and the Machine* collection." He smiled at her, and finished off his salmon.

Emma ran her finger around the rim of her wineglass and stared at him. "You're an interesting guy, Kyle Hadley. More so than I realized."

"Why thank you." Kyle knew people didn't think he was deep. Hell, he probably wasn't. But he did know he appreciated every day he was on earth, and he was appreciating having Emma Gideon across his kitchen table, a thoughtful smile on her face.

8

EMMA COULDN'T BELIEVE she was sitting at a bar with Ian Bainbridge himself. She had been barraging his camp with phone calls for a week and they had blown her off at every turn. One call from Kyle and here they were—a cozy foursome, chatting away like old friends. At least it appeared that Rosanna, Ian's assistant, and Kyle were getting cozy. She and Ian weren't having the same instant connection.

"So you're from New Zealand?" she asked Ian politely, attempting to break the ice.

To her left, Rosanna let out a peel of laughter at something Kyle said, and Emma tried not to grimace. She was starting to feel like she was on a double date, and hers was going badly. Kyle, the man she had just slept with the day before, appeared to be having a fabulous time, if the young and perky assistant's giggles were any indication. Determined not to glance their way, she shifted on her bar stool and smiled brightly at Ian. She was taking Kyle's approach to this conversation and not diving right in to questioning the photographer. She was going to ease into it and just try to be a friendly girl, not a journalist.

"Yes. I've been all over the world now, though. Haven't made it home in quite some time." He gave a rueful shrug and took a sip of his beer.

"I would imagine that's a bit of a trade-off for an artist. You have to travel, which is exciting, but you can't necessarily set down roots."

"The challenge of being an artist is that to be successful you have to be commercial, which goes against the grain of creativity. But that's not a conversation for a Monday with a lovely lady." He gave her a smile. "So is Kyle your boyfriend?"

"What? No. God. No." Emma blustered and then mentally kicked herself for giving such a heated reaction. "Why do you ask?" she added, trying very hard not to turn and look at Kyle.

"Because you keep glancing over at him, and I get the feeling that you basically would like to strangle Rosanna." Ian leaned closer to her. "I get that feeling myself sometimes. That giggle... God."

Emma laughed, disarmed by Ian's easy charm and by how he was clearly trying to make her feel more comfortable. "She's fine. And no, Kyle is not my boyfriend. We're coworkers and I suppose you could call us friends." She'd like to think they had gained ground in that respect. But for reasons she didn't quite understand, she wasn't going to go so far as to say that Rosanna could have at him. The very thought made her jealous, there was no denying it.

"You could say the same about Rosanna and me. She works hard and I appreciate that, but she is a flirt.

This ten-city shoot is making her giddy. Fresh blood in every town."

"More power to her," Emma said. "But that's so not me."

"Me, either. I'm not a casual hookup guy."

Emma was 99 percent sure Ian wasn't flirting with her in any way. He was an attractive guy, in his early thirties, with great bone structure and beautiful eyes. Yet he looked tired, like he wanted to retreat to New Zealand and sleep for about a month.

"Given that you've experienced a stalker, I can't imagine you'd want to hook up with strangers, anyway. You never know what you're going to get, and you do have celebrity cachet." Emma wasn't really commenting as a journalist. She was just commenting as a person. It would be scary to date after encountering a stalker. Hell, it was scary enough to date without a crazy following you around.

Ian set his beer down with a plunk and pushed up his black glasses with one finger. "It's absolutely ridiculous that I have a stalker. I mean, I could understand someone objecting to the nudity. Frankly, I expected that. But this person seems to think my photography is a kind of infidelity to her—and yet, we've never met. It's very bizarre."

"She thinks you're cheating on her by taking pictures of other women?"

"Yes. It's bonkers. I mean, first of all, I don't even know who she is, only that her name is Savannah. We don't have any sort of relationship whatsoever. But also, my work is not about exploiting women. I'm not doing it to get a view of some tits and ass. I'm making a statement."

Emma gripped the bar, trying not to appear too excited. The stalker's name was Savannah. How many Savannahs could there be? She realized Ian was indignant at having his motives questioned, but frankly, that didn't interest her. "Wow, that is really strange. I know the police are aware of what's going on, but have they gotten any leads as to who she is?"

"They haven't been much help because I move around so much that it's always a different police force. I almost think she's banking on no one putting much effort into learning her identity."

"Does she email you or write you letters?"

"Oh, yeah, I get emails all the time sent from public libraries with a variety of made-up email addresses. She alternates between telling me she loves me and reprimanding me for my fascination with women. It's a bit of an annoyance, but I really don't suspect she'll turn violent or anything. I just hope it doesn't result in a decrease in volunteer subjects."

"I don't think you need to worry about that. People enjoy being part of something big. Even I did it yesterday and I'm a total prude." Emma wondered if she could outright ask Ian for copies of those emails or if he would balk at the question.

"My agent insisted I hire a bodyguard. It's put a real dent in my privacy." Ian gave her a smile. "I ditched her tonight, so if you suddenly see me bugger out of here, it's because she's spotted me."

"Your bodyguard is a woman?"

He nodded. "Bit of a dragon, she is."

Rosanna leaned around her on the sticky bar and almost knocked Emma's wine over in an effort to reach her boss. "Can I have some quarters? Kyle and I are going to use the jukebox."

"What am I, your daddy? I don't have any quarters," Ian said. "And your hair is in Emma's wine. I imagine she'd like you to remove it."

Gross. It was. Glossy raven curls dipping down into her chardonnay. Rosanna's hair was beautiful, actually—the opposite of hers, which was straight and blond. Rosanna was also pin-thin, with no hips. Emma's jealousy boiled just a little hotter, much to her chagrin.

"I have quarters, we're good," Kyle said, standing up and fishing in his pocket.

"Yay!" Rosanna squealed as she grabbed Kyle's hand and pulled him away from the stools.

He shot Emma a bemused look.

She glared at him.

Which maybe she had no right to do, but really, the sheets should be cold—and changed—before he invited another woman into his bed. It was a little annoying to see him flirt with another woman so openly in front of her.

"She makes me feel quite stodgy and old," Ian said.

Considering she acted like she was twelve, Emma wasn't surprised. Instead, she tried to redirect the conversation to the stalker. "So I wonder why this Savannah person has fixated on you? What's the catalyst for a stalker? It's interesting."

Ian didn't look particularly interested in the motivations behind mentally ill fans. "Who knows? She mentioned that she worked in the pub I used to frequent in Pittsburgh. I don't remember ever meeting her, though."

Emma was making mental notes. It might actually be possible to track this girl down. "There wasn't anyone who specifically chatted with you about art or your photography?"

"I don't think so. But it was an eclectic neighborhood. Everyone there was pierced and into counterculture references."

"What was it called?"

For a second, Ian just looked at her, eyebrows raised, and she thought he was going to call her out on her motives. But if he knew her intent, he didn't say anything. "Church Street."

"Church Street? That's the name of the bar?"

"Yes." He gave her a genuine smile. "Hipsters only, you know."

"What? I'm not a hipster?" Emma smiled back. She was far from it. "And here I thought I had hipster down. I guess I need a tattoo or a piercing."

"A what?" Kyle asked, on his way back to his stool. "Don't you dare get a tattoo!"

Startled, Emma swiveled to glare at him. "Excuse me? I can get a tattoo if I want one." She didn't, necessarily, but it wasn't his right to offer an opinion, especially since Rosanna was clinging to his arm like a tight sweater.

Besides, he'd managed to interrupt the flow of her conversation with Ian. The man was volunteering information on his stalker, and Kyle was inserting himself into the dialogue.

Kyle added, "Are you ready to head out, Emma? I know you have an early morning tomorrow."

She did? It was just a Monday, a normal workday, and the last time she'd glanced at her phone, it wasn't even ten yet. Looking at him blankly, she tried to read his expression, but Kyle just looked his normal cheerful self. Was he trying to tell her something or was he merely expressing polite consideration for her?

"I'm fine," she told him, because she was.

"Are you sure? I know you're not much of a night owl."

What the hell was he talking about? He had no idea if she was a night owl or not. But she was starting to get the message loud and clear that he wanted to leave. Understanding dawned. He wanted to ditch her back at her car so he could go out with Rosanna.

She would not get angry. But she would dig her fingernails into her jeans and clench her teeth so tightly she was liable to chip one. The question was, did she give him what he wanted, or did she dig her heels in and ruin his plans of penetration? She couldn't decide whether to remain obstinate or prove to him she didn't care one iota by getting up and sailing out of the bar.

Ian spoke first. "We should probably head out, anyway. We're leaving on the bus in the morning for Chicago."

Kyle nodded sympathetically. "Understood. It was great to meet you, man. Thanks for coming out for a drink."

As he and Ian exchanged pleasantries, and Kyle insisted on picking up the tab, Emma realized Rosanna was glaring at her. "It must be fun to travel all over with Ian," Emma said politely, in an attempt at conversation.

"It's okay" was Rosanna's tepid answer. "But it's hard to meet people."

Ian seemed to think Rosanna met plenty of people,

but Emma kept her mouth shut. "That's a shame, but someday you'll be glad you got to see so much of the country."

"When I'm your age? Hopefully I won't have picked up the kind of weight you have."

Oh, hey now. Uncalled-for bitchiness. Emma felt her eyes widen. She had never learned how to deal with cattiness among girls. In college she'd been too busy studying journalism and finance to perfect the art of social criticism or backstabbing. She wasn't even sure what to say in response, but she did want this little girl to know she didn't intimidate her or hurt her feelings.

Then, like a divine gift from the goddess of gossip, she thought of an equally scathing response. So she just said calmly, "Exactly. And you'll probably look back and regret not using a condom when you really should have."

Okay, so maybe she did know how to play the game. Feeling like she'd just earned her sorority stripes, Emma tried not to smile.

Ian gave a choking laugh next to her.

Rosanna gasped in indignation. "What's your problem?"

"I don't have a problem. I really don't." Emma stood up and held her hand out to Ian. "It was a pleasure talking to you. We're going to give your shoot a nice write-up in the paper and it will run in Wednesday's edition. I'm looking forward to seeing the collection in its entirety when it's completed."

Ian shook her head. "Pleasure's all mine, Emma, and thank you. Enjoy the rest of your evening. You coming, Rosanna?"

"Well, that depends." She gave a pointed look at Kyle.

Kyle squeezed her hand. "Thanks for hanging out. This was fun even if you have lousy taste in music." He winked at her. "Enjoy Chicago."

Then he put his hand on the small of Emma's back and urged her toward the door. Emma barely had time to grab her purse and wave before they were outside. Irritated, she moved out of his touch the minute they hit the sidewalk. "What are you doing? I thought you wanted to go home with Rosanna."

He made a sound of exasperation. "No, I do not want to go home with Rosanna. I want to go home with you, and I'm fighting the feeling of total annoyance that you think I would bring you to a bar then ditch you for another woman."

Emma walked faster, trying to outpace both Kyle and her racing heart. She didn't like feeling jealous. It was so petty and small. "Well, you certainly seemed cozy enough with her."

"She was cozy with me, not the other way around. I was just being polite and friendly, not flirty. There is a difference. I figured there was no harm in it if I didn't encourage it further because it was giving you an opportunity to talk to Ian alone."

"Oh." It did sound plausible when he put it like that. Kyle was friendly. She knew that. She saw it every day at work. He didn't really flirt back. He just chatted. She thought back over the past hour and tried to analyze if he had actually flirted with Rosanna in any way, then was disgusted with herself for even going through the exercise. What difference did it make? They weren't dating.

But nonetheless, she thought when two people were sleeping together, they owed each other a little bit of courtesy and consideration. But they weren't sleeping with each other habitually. It had been a one-time deal. "This is why sleeping with you was a bad idea," she said. "It's already making me crazy and it's only been a day. Which we were supposed to pretend never happened."

"What is making you crazy? The idea that I would hook up with Rosanna? I would never do that. I'm not that kind of guy."

A quick glance showed he was frowning, his hands in his pockets.

Emma wasn't sure what to say. "Well, how am I supposed to know that?" she asked, feeling more than a little cranky.

"Maybe we should talk about a few things," he said, pulling his keys out and unlocking his car, which he'd parallel parked a few spots away from the bar.

Emma wasn't sure she wanted to talk if it involved pointing out that she was being irrational, which she knew she was. The night was warm, and her hair blew into her face. Tucking it behind her ears, Emma stopped walking and waited expectantly. "Like what?"

"The fact that you were jealous of Rosanna."

Emma blustered, but she couldn't really deny it. That didn't make it any less embarrassing.

"And the fact I was jealous of Ian."

That, however, shocked her. "You were? Why?"

"Because I thought he was hitting on you and it made me jealous. I don't want anyone to hit on you but me."

"You don't?" Not that she thought he actually wanted

her to hit on multiple men, but the point was, he was hinting at the fact that he cared. That it mattered to him who she flirted with and who she didn't. Jealousy didn't equate with a casual hookup they were both supposed to forget about and move on from.

Why did that suddenly make her so insanely happy?

KYLE SMILED AT the look on Emma's face. She was the picture of suspicion. "No, I don't." He had known earlier in the evening that he wanted to sleep with Emma again—many, many times, if she would let him—but he hadn't really thought about what dating her truly would mean until he had seen her talking and laughing with Ian Bainbridge. It had given him a tight pain in his chest, along with the sudden desire to punch things, and he had realized in astonishment that he was jealous. Which lead him to only one conclusion: he needed to see where this could go with Emma, for real.

Not just a casual date here and there, or random hookups. Not even the kind of litmus-test phase of early dating where they tested the waters to see if the relationship was working while still seeing other people. That clearly wasn't going to work here if he wanted to maintain his sanity.

There was something different here, something that made him feel very vested in seeing Emma smile, in wanting the right to touch her at will, a brush on her knee, a hand on the small of her back. He was enjoying getting to know her on a personal level, and he was starting to feel something that extended beyond a business association or even a first date.

He wanted to spend more time with Emma, in earnest.

So he tried to sound as sincere as he felt. "I was

wondering if you would be interested in dating me. You know, like seeing each other on a regular basis and not seeing other people. Just each other. Frequently."

"Are you serious?" She looked like a baby owl, her eyes were so big. "Do you really think that's a good idea? I mean, Claire…"

"Screw Claire," he said vehemently.

Emma's lip twitched. "I'd rather not."

He gave a nervous laugh. He hadn't realized how vested he was in her response. "Just leave Claire and anything else external out of the equation for a second. Do you want to spend time with me?" He felt mildly pathetic asking it that way, but he wanted to establish with certainty what they were doing.

"Yes," she said, though she didn't look thrilled about it.

But it was good enough for Kyle. "So does that mean we're dating? And we're not going to flirt with other people?"

"I guess."

He gave a light yank to the tips of her hair, both relieved and excited. "Don't sound so happy about it."

"I think we may be making a huge mistake," she said with the honesty he'd come to expect from her. "But I seem powerless to say no."

"That makes two of us."

She stepped into the car after he opened the door for her, and looked up at him, shaking her head. "How I went from I'm not going to sleep with you, to I'm going to sleep with you just once, to dating, is beyond me."

"I'm pretty irresistible." He grinned at her expression as he leaned over to kiss her through the open door, his lips lingering on the softness of her mouth.

"Actually, you're the one who is irresistible. I wasn't going to take no for an answer, so I think you were doomed. Sorry, but you're stuck with me now."

Kyle walked around the front of his car, maintaining eye contact with Emma through the windshield. God, she was so gorgeous. Even in just a plain white shirt and jeans, which had clearly been worn by her as some sort of neutral territory, neither work nor sexy times, she was just stunning. He had always thought so, but now when she looked at him with barely contained lust, he was damn near speechless at how hot she was.

In order to focus on driving and not send them careening into a ditch, Kyle forced himself to ask her about Ian. "So what did our photographer have to say?"

"He said he's gotten emails from the stalker. It's clearly motivated by a so-called love interest. But the amazing thing is, she signs her name. Who knows if it's a real name or not, but it's a name. Plus she told him they met at a bar in Pittsburgh. Of course he doesn't remember her."

"Interesting. That may be enough to go on. You should run with it." He wanted Emma to be successful at work. It clearly was so important to her, and if he could help her in any way, he was more than willing. Personally, he wanted to write interesting and well-researched articles and columns on a variety of subjects. That was enough for him to be satisfied with his job. But Emma wanted more, and he understood that.

"I won't be able to find anything in time for the article deadline tomorrow."

"Probably not," he agreed. "You should just go ahead and write it the way Claire wants it, without any mention of the stalker."

"Do you think so?" She bit the tender flesh of her bottom lip and he wanted to soothe her self-imposed injury with a soft kiss.

He settled for resting his free hand on her knee, giving it a squeeze through the denim of her jeans. "Yes, I do." For once, he didn't feel like making a crack or joke. He just wanted to enjoy the feeling of pleasure he got from Emma's company.

When they got back to his place, he was determined to make it out of the foyer before he pounced on Emma like a sex-crazed lunatic. Not that he wasn't around her, but he wanted to at least pretend he was rational, suave and in control.

"What kind of music do you like?" he asked her as he poured them both another glass of wine and brought it to her on the couch.

She gave him a smile. For once, she didn't look nervous and agitated. "I do like pop music, as you've seen from karaoke, but I have a secret love of big band and swing."

"I knew it." He kicked off his shoes and crossed his feet on the coffee table. He kept his place spotless, but that didn't mean he didn't like to be casual. Nothing was so precious that it couldn't be replaced.

Except for people.

That's what he had learned from his dad's passing.

"Your grandfather's influence?" he asked her.

"Yes." Emma stared into her wineglass, like she was conjuring up memories of good times past. "When I was little, I would stand on his feet, and he would dance with me."

"That's cute. So it was just you, your mom and your grandfather?"

She nodded. "My grandmother died before I was born. I think that's part of the reason my mom was a rebellious teen. She lost her mother at fifteen, and I think my grandfather was dealing with his own grief, and didn't know how to deal with hers, too. So she started skipping school and ignoring curfew. By eighteen she had moved out, and was pregnant with me."

"That will definitely make you grow up fast." Kyle was damn near thirty, and he couldn't imagine being a father yet. He wasn't ready to have someone rely on him for everything.

"It did. She was a great mother. She took naturally to it." Emma sipped her wine and put it down. "What about your mother? Is she the one who taught you to be a neat freak?"

"A neat freak?" Kyle frowned in mock offense. "If I were a neat freak, I would be cringing right now over the fact you set that wine down without a coaster."

Her eyes widened and she picked her glass up. "Oh, sorry!"

He laughed. "I'm not the least bit bothered by it. I don't care. I do like a clean house, but that's probably more because my brother Andrew was a disgusting pig and I had to share a room with him. But it's not a compulsion, just a preference."

"I bet you made your bed today. After I ran out of here leaving towels all over your bathroom." She moistened her lips, clearly remembering what they had done in the shower. "I'm such a lousy houseguest."

He felt his cock swell in response to the stimulus she was unwittingly providing. "I'll forgive you. I'll even let you rumple my sheets all over again."

That drew a sly smile from her. "Oh, you're too kind. Should we retire to the bedroom, then?"

"Yes. Let's." He stood up, amused as always by her formal forties language. "Though I do believe this might fall under the heading of Funny Business."

"I think I can retract my earlier statement. I do believe changing her mind is a woman's prerogative."

He wasn't going to argue with that, especially not when it worked in his favor.

KYLE HELD HIS hand out for her and she accepted it, anticipation running high. She knew what he was capable of doing to her body. What she hadn't realized was what he was capable of doing to her head. She felt more relaxed, at ease, than she had in months, and it was from his easy company and casual but thoughtful conversation.

Emma felt like he had opened a door and she had walked through it, without any real understanding of where it led to. But that was half the excitement.

He took her breath away, and for a woman who sometimes forgot to breathe, that was a definite mark in his favor.

Once they were in his room, he pulled his phone out of his pocket and made a few swipes with his thumb. Suddenly Frank Sinatra was crooning in the dark room.

That was how he disarmed her, and Emma couldn't help but smile. "Nice touch," she told him, kicking her shoes off by his dresser.

He set the phone down and held out his hand again. "May I have this dance?"

"You want me to dance?" She enjoyed that he wasn't afraid to try something, wasn't concerned he might fall flat, or be perceived as corny. He just went with his instinct, without pausing to analyze it from seventeen different angles. She appreciated it, and needed to absorb a little of that behavior from him.

But she didn't want to think about self-improvement at the moment. She just wanted to enjoy the fact that a very gorgeous man had just asked her to dance in a dark room, his bed mere feet away.

"Yes, I want to dance with you. I can't guarantee it will be much more than swaying on our feet, but I'd like to feel you in my arms."

Oh, God. He knew exactly the right thing to say to her. It was romantic, the way he pulled her close against him, and Emma felt herself succumbing to his charms. She had never thought she was a girl who needed flowers and poetry, but at the moment, she wouldn't trade her hands on his chest while they moved with the music for anything.

Then he kissed her.

She already knew the contours of his body intimately, but there was something different about this, about drawing out the anticipation, about exploring each other slowly and intently with hands and mouths, hips rocking together with the music. Frank Sinatra happened to be one of her favorites, because who could resist Ol' Blue Eyes? His voice was always a mix of amused and amorous, which arguably described Kyle, as well.

No wonder she was such a sucker for him.

His tongue trailed across her bottom lip and their breathing deepened, their bodies melding together as they danced.

Kyle stepped back and peeled off his shirt.

Emma did the same. They drew back together, not needing the words to know they both wanted to feel the heat of each other's skin intimately connected. Kyle unhooked her bra with a deft flick of his fingers against her back, and she shifted so she could divest herself completely of it. Then, still swaying to the music, she locked eyes with him and unbuttoned her jeans. His eyes narrowed in the ribbon of light coming from the hallway, and he popped the button on his own pants.

"You're so beautiful," he told her.

Under his intense gaze, she felt beautiful. "Thank you." She couldn't really begin to describe to him how gorgeous she thought he was, so she didn't bother. She just slipped out of her jeans and her panties, until she stood before him completely naked.

Kyle pulled back the comforter with one hard yank, then gave her a gentle tug over to the bed. He pushed her down on it, her back sinking into the softness of the mattress, legs dangling over the edge. Then he kissed her clitoris and proceeded to make love to her with his tongue repeatedly, until she had come three times and reached for him in silent plea.

There was something different between them, something quieter, stronger, the passion just as deep and intense, but now laced with something more that she didn't quite understand. It made every stroke of him inside her resonate with the pleasure and importance of a threshold crossed.

"I can't..." he panted. "I can't hold off anymore."

"You don't need to," she told him. She knew that when he came, she would, too. She could already feel what he was doing to her, building up the tension inside her, knowing it would release in their mutual gratification.

"Emma," he said, and then they were there. Together.

She closed her eyes and fell over the edge, in more ways than one.

9

EMMA FLOATED INTO work on a high of sexual endorphins and career promise.

It took only one spilled coffee and Claire to ruin her mood.

She was searching online for the bar in Pittsburgh called Church Street when she heard Claire's voice bark at her from a few feet away. "Gideon, in my office. Now."

Emma jumped and spilled her coffee in her lap. On her white skirt.

"Damn." She glanced at it ruefully, but quickly closed her browser before Claire saw what she was doing, given that pursuing the stalker angle wasn't exactly what she was supposed to be working on. At all.

Standing up, she looked around her desk for napkins to magically appear, but when none did, she just gave up on the stain and followed Claire, who had already marched off in the direction of her corner office, which had sweeping views of downtown. Emma's cube had sweeping views of the door to the men's restroom, which was a precarious position to be in after lunch each afternoon.

"Shut the door," Claire said in a tone that made Emma nervous.

She did as she was told and hovered in front of Claire's desk. Her boss spun her monitor around so Emma could see that Claire had been reading the article she'd submitted that morning on the photo shoot, with only a brief mention of the disappearance of the clothes. Unsure why Claire looked like she had a severe case of constipation, Emma just stood and waited, her palms slick with sweat.

"Is this your story?"

"Yes." Did she think she plagiarized it?

"There's nothing in this article. It's 250 words of nothing."

That had been precisely why she had wanted to add the stalker angle, but Emma remained silent. From experience, she knew Claire wasn't finished.

"Kyle mentioned you had drinks with Ian Bainbridge last night."

"Yes." Her heart picked up its pace. Why would Kyle tell Claire that? And why did it matter?

"You were pressing him for information on his stupid stalker, weren't you?"

"No." She hadn't been. Not really. It had been more of a *conversation* than an interview, technically. Had Claire gotten a complaint call from Ian? He hadn't seemed annoyed, but you never knew when it came to artists.

"Did you ask him about it?"

"Sure. He actually offered a pretty solid lead that I don't think the police have ever followed up on."

"Did you ask him about his future plans after he's done with this collection?"

Whoops. "No."

"Did you ask him about the impact of digital technology on his art? Now that people can zoom in on the internet and identify individuals, has there been any backlash from employers? Has he had problems with copyright infringement?"

Uh-oh. Now she really knew she had screwed up royally. "No."

"Does he feel that he's found acceptance from the art world?"

"I don't know."

Claire looked furious, and Emma felt like an idiot. Maybe her focus had been a little too narrow. To say the least.

"I'm not running this," Claire said, with a wave of her hand at the computer. "And you're on unofficial probation. I've never seen you make such an error in judgment."

"Probation? Are you serious?" Emma felt her stomach go sour, and panic caught her in its grip. She wanted a promotion, not to be on probation. Probation was for criminals who were released from jail. For slackers and overall losers. Not her. Feeling like she was about to faint, Emma swallowed hard.

"Yes. You need to stop trying to be the star reporter and just do your job. Unless you can accept that it is what it is and that you need to listen to me, we're going to have a problem."

"We don't have a problem," Emma insisted. "I understand." She understood that she had made a huge mistake.

"This is Life & Style. You should have been focusing on *art* and nothing else. Now get out of here before I really get pissed."

Emma didn't need to be told twice, though she did force a few words past the giant lump crowding her throat. "I'm sorry. I wasn't trying to be insubordinate. I just thought that criminal activity was worth including in this story."

Claire's expression softened a tad. "Look, I know you're good at what you do. But ease up on the Woodward and Bernstein routine. It's not doing you any favors."

"Okay. Thanks." Not that she wanted to thank Claire for anything, but she wasn't sure what else to say. Pivoting on her heel, she made her way back to her cubicle, where she sank down into her chair, shaking, the damp spot on her skirt sticking to her leg.

"Hey, want to go to lunch?" Kyle asked, a picture of casual cheer as he came up behind her.

"Won't people think that's weird?" she asked, suddenly feeling overwhelmed by Claire's ire. The last thing in the world she needed was to have the fact that she was dating Kyle become common knowledge.

He shrugged, but before he could respond, she swiveled her chair around and studied his face, feeling more shocked than angry. She couldn't believe that in the course of just a few days, her entire career seemed to have been derailed. "Why did you tell Claire we met Ian Bainbridge last night?"

"I thought we could get an extension on your story.

I didn't tell her I was there at all. I just said you mentioned that you'd interviewed him."

There was nothing in that she could fault Kyle for. Nodding, she said, "Well, Claire has put me on probation. She thinks I'm focusing on the wrong priorities."

"What?" Kyle looked stunned. "That's bullshit."

Emma glanced around the office, but no one was looking in their direction. "Shh. No, she probably has a point. I tend to fixate, and in this case, I chose the wrong thing to fixate on. I just need to make sure I'm completely toeing the line and don't screw up in any way." Which meant no hints of misconduct. "I don't think lunch is a good idea."

He frowned, but he didn't protest. "Well, this sucks." His voice lowered. "Can I see you Friday?"

She nodded, but added, "Just text me. We shouldn't be talking any more at work. We never did before." Feeling like a kid about to get caught for swiping a cookie, Emma turned around and picked up her phone. She started pushing buttons at random like she was making a call as he moved away.

She was terrible at subterfuge.

Her phone dinged. She had a text already from Kyle. He must have been typing as he walked away.

Am I your dirty little secret?

She smiled despite the crappiness of the day.

I wouldn't say little.

He sent a little devil emoticon back.
Then another message immediately.

You're my sexy secret. I can't wait to...

Emma waited but he didn't finish his sentence. She couldn't resist. She typed.

Can't wait to what?

Sing with you again.

That brought a giggle to her lips before she could prevent it.

"What's so funny over there?" Sandy asked her, head popping over the top of the divider. "If it's a dirty joke, you must share."

"It's nothing."

"You're sexting with a guy, aren't you?"

Despite her cheeks heating, Emma scoffed at Sandy. "No, of course not."

But she did write back to Kyle.

I could sing all night with you.

If she were going to get fired, at least she would also be getting laid.

She wasn't sure if that was comforting or not.

IT WASN'T COMFORTING since Kyle didn't seem particularly concerned about getting caught. Not only had he spent the week cruising by her cubicle to say a word or two here and there, something he'd never done before, but he showed up at the food festival Emma was covering for the paper.

It was a beautiful summer night, in the low seventies, and the aroma of dozens of food booths was in the air. Emma was carrying her tablet to take pictures for the paper and was wandering around in her work clothes, but with carefree flip-flops underneath, when her phone buzzed with a text from Kyle.

Where are you at?

The food festival.

What booth?

Emma glanced around and texted back.

Gyros.

What was he up to?

It was obvious a second later when he appeared next to her, the crowd parting to reveal his sauntering walk and his smug smile. "Hey."

"What are you doing here?" she asked, unable to prevent herself from smiling back. He was so cute, his tie loosened, the sleeves of his dress shirt rolled up. They were overdressed for the festival, but Emma had come straight from the office, which was only a block away, and clearly Kyle had done the same.

"I was hungry." He leaned over and kissed her. "And I missed you."

Yeah, that was him not caring in the slightest if they got caught. Emma glanced around nervously, but at the same time, his words made her feel giddy. It was impossible to be angry with a man when his only crime was wanting to pay attention to you. "I just saw you at work. It's been twenty minutes."

"That's not the same. It's making me feel twitchy to be around you, but I can't touch you." Kyle laced his fingers through hers.

Emma was amazed at how natural it felt. "I know. I keep wanting to tell you things, to ask your opinion, and it's weird that I can't."

"So that's why I'm here. If someone sees me, we can say we just ran into each other."

"And our hands fell together?" Emma laughed, feeling lighter and freer than she had in years. She should be worried, but she wasn't, and it felt fantastic.

"It could happen." He shrugged and gave her a grin. "Plus I really am hungry. What looks good to you?"

"Everything. There's a whole row of rib booths, there's a taco truck, and pierogies, of course. Though to be honest, I was really eyeing the cupcake booth."

"So you have a sweet tooth?"

She nodded. "Oh, yeah. More like a sweet mouth."

That didn't sound quite right. Kyle's eyebrows went up and down. "That's what I was thinking."

She laughed. "I meant that it's not just one tooth that craves sweets. It's every tooth, like a whole mouthful. Never mind. Suffice it to say I really like sugar."

"I'm more a salt lover myself. But now I know how to bribe you."

As they strolled down the center aisle checking out the options, Emma marveled at how easy it was to be with Kyle, how natural it felt. The sun was on her face. Her hair was pulled back into a loose ponytail, her toes happy and free of her usual pumps. Maybe there was a way to balance work with pleasure.

"I think I want to start with a Coney dog. Do you mind if I get onions?" he asked.

"You're going to start with a Coney? What are you going to follow that up with, besides antacids?" The thought made her stomach clench. "Of course you can have onions if you want them."

"I don't want you to refuse to make out with me. And a Coney is just a warm-up. From there I think I'll move on to a slab of ribs, then one of those fancy wrap things." He pointed to an Asian fusion booth.

"You were serious about being hungry."

"I'm a growing boy. I need to keep my strength up." He smiled at her. "Speaking of which, can you come home with me tonight? I was hoping you'd be my dessert."

"On a work night?" she asked, panic immediately springing up.

"On a work night, yes," he told her solemnly. "It's scandalous, I know. But I can have you in bed by eight, I promise."

That made her fight the urge to smile. "Really? How thoughtful of you."

"I try. So I'll take that as a yes."

He was too charming to resist. "I'll need to stop at home and get some clothes for tomorrow. Plus pj's to wear to bed."

"Of course you'll need work clothes. But I think you can skip the pj's. Save yourself the extra laundry and sleep naked. That's my plan."

Emma rolled her eyes, but she couldn't prevent her smile. This felt good, easy, right. Planning a sleepover with Kyle Hadley? Who would have thought.

Ten minutes later they were sitting on a bench in

the sun, Kyle with a full spread of food balanced on his lap, Emma with a Panini. As they ate, Kyle talked about growing up the youngest of three boys.

"We all played sports," he told her. "I think my mother spent ten years sitting on bleachers watching different games. I don't know how she did it."

"My mom worked a lot," Emma said. "I took dance lessons rather unsuccessfully, but I did love it. My grandfather always took me. He would read the paper while he waited for me and he would clip out the comics and leave them next to my breakfast plate every morning." Emma pulled a French fry out of her sandwich. "He definitely influenced my love of journalism. He was always reading the paper. What made you chose this field?"

Kyle gave her a rueful smile, his Coney in his hand. "To be honest, I kind of fell into it. I got a communications degree in college, because well, I like to talk, and because I wasn't sure what else to do. Then I went to a career fair my senior year and got hired on the spot by a trade paper. I discovered I really liked writing."

"Networking comes naturally to you," she said, for once not feeling jealous of that. "It's a good fit."

"And you're tenacious, which makes it a good fit for you."

"Thank you," she said, sincerely. She nibbled her French fry and felt more relaxed than she had in…ever.

Kyle swiped one of her fries. She laughed. "Don't you have enough food? You need to steal mine?"

"I couldn't resist. You have that effect on me."

This time when he leaned in for a kiss, Emma didn't even think to worry who was watching. She just tilted her head and met him halfway.

KYLE PEELED OFF his shirt and attacked the dilapidated fence with vigor. His mom had been looking to replace the rotting wood at the back of her property for years and he and his two brothers had finally managed to find a Saturday morning they were all free to do it. He hadn't gotten much sleep the night before, due to the fact that Emma had been fairly insatiable in bed, but he wasn't about to complain about it.

"Showing off, huh?" his brother Jason ribbed him. "Pretty muscles, pretty boy."

"Suck it," he told him, because that's what you said to your brother. As the youngest, he'd taken a fair share of teasing over the years. It had probably contributed to his calm demeanor. He let words roll off him, and hell, he knew his brothers messed with him because it was the way they showed they cared. Both Jason and Andrew were married to great girls, and Jason had two kids, while Andrew had one on the way.

"Hot date last night?" Andrew asked him. "You look whipped."

He grinned as he tore down a section of fencing with his hands, encased in work gloves. "As a matter of fact..."

"I don't want to hear this," Jason said. "It will make me lament the loss of my bachelor days. Last night I was in bed by ten. My wife was in bed by nine-freaking-thirty. Then Jace woke us up at two crying because his binky fell out of his mouth. Those are my hot Friday nights now."

His brother was stacking the boards Kyle was pulling off onto a tarp to drag to the curb. He shook his head ruefully.

"Tell me about it," Andrew said. "Katie is one giant

ball of bitchy. Plus she's so pregnant she burps all the time. I keep thinking wow, I really love this woman so much, and I'm so happy, but it's a hell of a lot different from five years ago when we were out partying and then having wild monkey sex all night. I'm looking forward to our daughter being born, but man, I miss the monkey sex."

Andrew was the tallest of the three of them, topping out at nearly six-five, and Kyle suddenly had a horrible vision of him leaping around Katie in the bedroom. "Can we not talk about anyone's sex life, please? I'm getting a visual I do not need and I just ate breakfast." Sweat rolled down between his shoulder blades as he yanked another length of fencing.

"So what you're saying is she turned you down."

He wasn't falling for that. "I'm not saying anything one way or the other." Though he couldn't help but grin when he thought about Emma yanking his shirt off in a fit of passion.

"What's her name?"

"Emma."

For some reason, both his brothers laughed.

"What?" he asked, mystified.

"You should have heard yourself, man. The way you said her name." Jason batted his eyelashes and started fluttering his hands in what was supposed to be a feminine gesture. *"Emma. Oh, Emma."*

Andrew got in on the action. "Kiss me, Kyle, you big stud." He pursed his lips and made smooch sounds.

Embarrassed, but mostly because his brothers were such idiots, Kyle shook his head. "You're douche bags. Thirty-five-year-old peckerheads."

So he liked Emma. Big deal.

But he had a feeling it was a bigger deal than he was ready to admit.

There was actually something to be said for the fact they couldn't be open about their relationship, because it just might be more than he could handle. He had never felt this way about a woman, and it was frightening. Even his college love had been based more on a lustful attraction than anything else. It had been obsessive and all-consuming. This was different. It was a first for him to have a budding friendship with a woman that was running parallel to a very fulfilling sexual relationship, and he wasn't exactly sure how to proceed.

It had to go somewhere, didn't it? Or did it? That was the question he was grappling with.

Concentrating on tearing down the wood, feeling the burn in his biceps and the strain in his shoulders, Kyle asked, "So how do you know when a woman is one you should, you know, commit to?"

His brothers both stopped laughing.

"Dude, for real?" Jason asked, concern in his voice.

Kyle nodded.

"You just know," Andrew said. He clapped him on the shoulder. "Don't overthink it. Just let it happen."

That wasn't exactly illuminating advice.

Katie came across the yard, waddling in the way only a woman nine months pregnant can. She was wearing what looked like a feed sack to Kyle, but was really just the ugliest maternity dress he'd ever seen.

"Do you guys want some beer?" she asked, then followed her question up with an extremely loud burp.

Kyle and Jason laughed.

"Babe," Andrew said. "It sounds like you've already been drinking."

"I can't help it!" Then she glanced at Kyle. "Your phone is blowing up with texts from someone named Foxy Emma. I wasn't being nosy, but it was on the kitchen counter and the name caught my attention."

His brothers snickered. Kyle just said, "Thanks," and refused to explain.

Instead he just kicked the fencing hard to feel manly again.

EMMA HELD A squirming dachshund and tried to focus on what her mother was saying. But between the yipping of dogs all around, the slippery maneuvers of the dog in her arms and the fact that Kyle hadn't answered a single one of her texts, Emma was struggling.

"Mom, can I put him down?" She was holding Elton John, her mother's three-year-old wiener dog.

"No. He doesn't play well with others." Her mother was calmly bent over to brush her other two dachshunds, both female, clearly enjoying the chaos of the annual wiener dog races at the fairgrounds.

"Then why did we bring him?" Emma asked.

"So he can watch the girls race."

"The girls" referred to the chocolate-brown shorthairs she was brushing, Madonna and Cher, who both looked like the only racing they did was to the food bowl. They were plumper than a vet would probably deem healthy, but then again, her mother was a little heavier than her GP approved of. Over the years, her mom had added a few pounds at a time to her frame until she had rounded out and softened. She was still beautiful. She just didn't have time for exercise or diets.

As far as Emma could tell, she ate healthy—plenty of veggies and lean meats—though she did have a sweet tooth.

Emma figured she was looking at her own body shape in twenty years and she was fine with that. Her mother oozed confidence and knew how to dress to emphasize every curve in the best way possible. At the moment, she wore tight stretch jeans with a black cotton shirt, belted to show off her narrow natural waist. She had on black Keds and dangling dachshund earrings, hanging below her sassy blond pixie haircut. The blond was no longer natural, but the smile always was.

"I think he just wants to go to the bratwurst stand." Emma couldn't believe how many food stands there were, how many things were being fried in the summer heat. The temperature had ballooned into the high eighties and Emma was sweating in her shorts and T-shirt.

"I can't believe they're selling hot dogs at a wiener-dog race. It just seems offensive," her mother said.

"Well, technically this is the German-American festival so I guess they didn't take into consideration how a wiener dog might feel about it." She gripped Elton John tighter as he shook his head, trying to break free. "When does the race start?"

"At noon." Her mother gave her an assessing look. "Do you have somewhere to be, honey? You didn't have to come. I could have asked Buck to help me with the dogs."

Emma liked Buck, her mother's boyfriend, but she was grateful for some time alone with her mom. "No, no, it's fine. I want to spend time with you."

She did. Talking to Kyle had reminded her how

precious time could be, and she wanted to enjoy her mother's company so she had jumped at her mom's suggestion to come to the festival. She just wished Elton would settle down. "What are their chances? How did they place last year?"

"Madonna got third out of twenty dogs. She's competitive. But Cher took her time. She doesn't give a hoot what people think of her."

Good Lord, her mother could be describing her and Kyle instead of a couple of dogs. "I think I'm more like Madonna."

"I know," her mother said ruefully. "I could never figure out where that came from because it sure wasn't from me. How many times when you were little did I tell you to just slow down and enjoy yourself?"

"A lot," she admitted. "And actually, if I'm a little distracted, it's because I screwed up at work."

"Doing what? You never make a misstep at work."

"Well, this time I did." Emma still got a cold chill when she thought about her conversation with Claire. She jiggled Elton John, hoping to stun him into compliance. "This photographer who was in town last week, you know, from the seminude photo shoot? Well, I was supposed to just do a standard write-up and I got caught up in the story of him having a stalker. I wanted to see if I could identify the stalker, maybe tie the piece into the lack of effectiveness of anti-stalker laws when stalkers cross state lines, but my editor told me to drop it."

"Yeah? So what happened?" Her mother stood back up, watching her with concern.

"I went and interviewed the guy, but when Claire

found out, she was furious. I didn't get more details about the photographer's future plans, his work, you know—information that people who read the entertainment section would be interested in. Instead I wasted the opportunity by asking him about his stalker." She had. It was painful to admit, but it was the truth. "So Claire ripped me a new one, and it's stressing me out."

"I'm sure it's just a blip."

"But I keep thinking that if I could just find out the stalker's identity it would prove my point. Which is the last thing I should be trying to do. I should be keeping my mouth shut and just doing what Claire tells me to do, which is covering the reopening of the contemporary art museum in two weeks at its new location."

"Is this stalker dangerous?"

"I think she could be. Honestly, I do. It may be accidental, but messing around with his photo-shoot sites when there are hundreds of volunteers involved has the potential to be dangerous."

"Then you know you have to do what's right. Screw what your boss thinks." Her mother smoothed her worn hands over the backs of the dogs, her calluses hard-earned from years and years of cleaning other people's houses. "You don't even have to run the story in the paper if your boss doesn't like it. But if you can expose her identity, you can at least tell the police."

Her mother was right. "That's a damn good point, Mom." Maybe that was why she hadn't been able to push her conversation with Ian out of her head. If she had the opportunity to potentially stop a criminal, she should. Plain and simple. It didn't have to affect her job in any way.

"So are you seeing anyone?" her mom asked, totally off topic.

Or was it? Because Kyle, on the other hand, definitely had the ability to affect her job, and not in a good way. "I sort of am." She hedged a little because it was new, and she was already falling faster than she should. Maybe if she downplayed it, it would temper her feelings.

"Oh, really? Who is the lucky guy?"

"Kyle Hadley. I work with him, so it's hush-hush. Claire wouldn't like that, either."

"Claire doesn't like much, does she?"

Emma laughed. "No." Then she chewed her bottom lip, getting serious again as she thought about the very real ramifications. "Do you think it's stupid to date him if my boss doesn't like it?"

"Do you have fun with him? Does he make you laugh?"

"Definitely."

"Is there chemistry between you?"

She could answer that without hesitation, as well. "Oh, yes. We have a ton of chemistry."

"Then don't let an employer dictate what you do in your free time. It took me twenty years to find a man as decent as Buck. Life is too short and a good man too hard to find to let an uptight boss interfere."

Emma nodded. The funny thing was, most people would put her in the same uptight camp as Claire. The thought didn't sit well. But she shoved it aside when she realized the race was about to start.

"Look, they're lining up."

Half a dozen dachshunds wearing numbers on their backs were waddling over to the starting line. Her mother led Madonna and Cher over before removing their leashes.

"Go to the finish line, Emma, and encourage them."

Only for her mother.

She dropped Elton John to the ground, regardless of his inability to keep it together around other dogs. Her arms were aching and he was a determined little contortionist. He jogged lightly beside her while she held his leash in an iron grip in case he decided to dash over to another dog and start trouble. But he held it together just fine and when they joined the other people at the finish line, Emma had to admit, the wieners racing were pretty darned cute. They tottered along the raceway, dashing toward their owners and the treats that were waiting at the finish line. One tripped, and another one jumped on the dog next to him, but for the most part, they seemed to know what they were doing.

Madonna was bounding to the finish neck and neck with the longhair to her right. She came in a narrow second with a camera finish. Even Elton John let out a bark of excitement.

"Yay, Madonna!" Emma cheered and bent down and rubbed her head. Elton John licked her.

Cher ambled along, stopping for a potty break at the halfway point. Generally speaking, she looked pretty pleased with herself even though she came in dead last.

Laughing, Emma figured there was a life lesson somewhere in all of this.

Everyone had to take the path that was right for him or her.

Emma knew she had to do the right thing, and that was to catch a stalker if she could.

Her phone beeped and she saw it was a text from Kyle.

Sorry for not answering sooner, babe. Working in Mom's yard. Miss you, foxy lady.

Emma grinned and tucked her phone away. She was going to continue to see Kyle, even if she had to hide it.

10

KYLE WAS SURPRISED at how quickly he and Emma slid into a dating routine. During the week, they usually only saw each other at work and maybe one night for a bite to eat. But on Fridays, he cooked dinner for them, then sometimes they went to karaoke, before tearing up the sheets at his place. On Saturdays, they did something outdoors together, split for a few hours to do various errands and meet family and friend commitments solo, then were together again in time for a movie or some other form of Saturday night entertainment before yet another night of passion at Emma's apartment.

Sundays were for sleeping in, French toast and then walking her mother's goofy dogs. He'd met Emma's mom, Rhonda, and he really liked her. The only lousy spots to their summer weekends were Sunday nights, when Emma insisted he go home so she could get a decent night's sleep before work. Though he understood, because even after a month of dating he still couldn't get enough of her body—and they didn't get a lot of sleep on the weekends—it was getting harder and harder to drag himself away and go home to an empty bed.

Emma didn't seem bothered by it. She definitely needed her space a little more than he did, which was ironic. He would have thought he would be the one who was itching for time with the boys, but truthfully he just wanted to hang out with Emma on the weekends. Where she was bothered and he wasn't, was their work arrangement. It was grinding on her that their relationship was a secret from their coworkers, and yet, for whatever reason, that wasn't hard for him to cope with.

In a way, it made it kind of exciting that he had to pretend he didn't know every single inch of Emma's glorious body. But to her, it was a strain to lie.

Sure, he figured eventually the truth was bound to come out, but for now, for the rest of the summer, he was content to do what they were doing. It was all sunshine and orgasms as far as he was concerned.

He jogged up the steps to her third-floor apartment, whistling, wearing cargo shorts and a T-shirt. After they walked the dogs, they were going to a ball game and he was excited to see the current pitching roster in action.

"Come in!" she said when he knocked.

Emma's apartment initially had surprised him. He had expected it to be neat and organized, the way her space at work was. It certainly wasn't messy or dirty, but there was a large amount of stuff everywhere. She seemed to collect all manner of random things, from hats to teacups to little tiny spoons hanging on the kitchen wall. It had been visually overwhelming to him at first, but once he'd gotten used to it, it felt homey and comfortable. Her mother spent Sundays with her boyfriend, Buck, on his boat out on the lake so she brought her three dogs to Emma's.

In the beginning, he wasn't sure how he felt about a trio of wiener dogs, but he had to admit, he was growing attached to the little furballs. They came running over to him when he opened the door and walked in. "Hey, guys, what's up?"

He went down in a squat to greet them. Madonna was so excited she was jumping up and down and running in circles around him. Elton John licked his leg repeatedly while Cher took her sweet time ambling over to him. Having a brother who was allergic, he hadn't grown up with dogs and he was constantly amazed at how clearly distinct each of their personalities were. He passed out head rubs all around and tugged on the toy ball Madonna gripped in her mouth.

Emma came out wearing a heart-stopping tank top and little denim shorts that made him want to drop something so she would bend over. He gave a low whistle. "Hey, baby. I think we should go to baseball games more often if that's how you're going to dress," he told her, standing up so he could go and attack her lips with his.

She laughed, pushing his hands off her breasts when he tried to grope them. "It's hot out."

"It's hot in here." Kyle went for her waist again, determined to pull her up against him. "Let's take our clothes off."

"We already bought the tickets," she said, darting out of his reach and smiling at him. "We don't want to miss the kickoff."

He wasn't even going to comment on her lack of understanding of baseball terminology. Kyle just liked when Emma smiled at him. It made him feel truly, deeply happy.

He thought of his brothers taunting him, and he wondered if he was as far gone as they seemed to think he was. Emma handed him Elton John's leash, and he realized he had the answer to that question. He was getting poetic about her freakin' smile while walking her mother's roly-poly dogs. He was gone all right. Like a fastball flying straight out of the park.

Going, going, gone.

WHEN KYLE LOOKED at her like that, Emma lost all ability to think rationally. She thought that should be a problem, but so far, she was choosing to ignore it. She was just basking in it. The past few weeks with him had been the most fun she'd had in years. She relaxed around him. She laughed. Her biggest fear, that she would feel insecure because he was so good-looking and such a flirt, hadn't been realized because his focus was always on her.

He was thoughtful and considerate, and hell, he was willing to walk her mother's dogs with her. That was a man who had her back. They were in harmony every weekend with how to spend their time together, and while they had dissimilar personalities, they had similar tastes and views.

The only thing that bothered her was lying about it at work. It wasn't in her nature to be dishonest, and while Kyle saw it as simply being private, she saw it as something more ominous. It felt wrong to be withholding the new reality of her life with him from the entire office. Not to mention she would kind of like to gush and brag a little about how super awesome he was and how mega happy she was. Wasn't that a girl's right? Especially a girl who hadn't dated in over a year. She should be allowed to wear her relationship on her sleeve, not have to hide it.

Plus there was the little matter of never having told him that she had actually spent some time poking into Ian Bainbridge's stalker and was 99 percent sure she knew her identity. She wasn't sure what Kyle's reaction to that would be, given she was on probation at work, and she wasn't sure what she should do with the information. So for the moment, she was ignoring it.

"Down, Cher!" Emma said to the dog, who was inappropriately making use of Kyle's leg.

He just laughed. "At least someone is willing to hump me."

"I'm willing," she told him, grabbing her keys off the counter. "Just not right now."

"That's what they all say." Kyle gave a mock sigh, but he followed her out of the apartment and down the cracked sidewalk, two dogs to her one.

She tended to walk Cher, because she refused to walk in harmony with either of the other dogs and it usually resulted in a tangled leash mess. Kyle walked Madonna and Elton John on the right, she had Cher on the left, and it worked. It was definitely a scorcher of a summer day, though, and she shoved her sunglasses on her head as the blinding sun hit her eyes. She lived in an older neighborhood, a mixed blend of houses and apartment buildings, with big leafy trees and uneven sidewalks. People rode their bikes and walked dogs on a regular basis, and she enjoyed the family feel of it.

A preteen on a skateboard whizzed past them on the street, his jeans tight and purple, his hair in his eyes. It was easy to feel contented on a day, a walk, like this.

"How did the fence go?" she asked. She had yet to meet his mother or his brothers, and she was starting to wonder if and when that would happen. It felt like she and Kyle were moving toward something in their relationship, but she wasn't sure. She tried not to worry about it, but let's face it, she was both a woman and a neurotic. She was doomed to spend at least a marginal amount of time pondering the future course of their relationship.

"Good. We're finally finished installing the new one. It took longer than I thought it would, but at least we got it done before my sister-in-law had her baby, because then we would have lost Andrew's help. She's a week past due and looks ready to pop."

"Does she know what she's having?" Emma hadn't spent a lot of time around babies. Whenever she saw one going by in a stroller, she marveled at the amazing oddities they were. She couldn't picture herself having one anytime soon, and was reminded again how much she owed her mother.

"It's a girl. My brother was supposed to keep it a secret, but he spilled the beans by accident. He made a casual comment about being outnumbered by females in his house and that was it. My mom started crying, Katie hit him. You know how it goes."

Actually, she didn't. "Not really. It's the only-child thing. But I don't get it, why does the sex of the baby have to be a secret?" She tugged on Cher's leash to get her out of the bush she was currently lumbering through in her neighbor's yard.

And why did it seem like she was constantly being reminded of secrets?

Guilt, that's why.

She was worried about what would happen if Claire discovered she and Kyle were involved. Because what was she without her job at the paper? She didn't know and it scared her. Losing everything she had worked so hard for was terrifying, yet it wasn't stopping her from continuing to see Kyle. And that was even more terrifying.

"You're asking the wrong guy. I have no idea." He grinned at her. "I mean it's a fifty-fifty chance it's one or the other."

That deserved an eye roll, which she gave him. He expected it, of course. It was part of their repertoire. He joked and teased and she pretended disdain. "Do they have a name picked out?"

"Yeah, but I don't remember what it was. It was something like Lauren or Jessica or Ashley. But I can say for certain it wasn't anything unusual. I would name my daughter something interesting, if I ever have one."

"Like what?" Picking at the front of her tank top, Emma wondered if they should cut the walk short. She was sweating in unpleasant places.

"Titania. Pocahontas. Aramathea."

Emma stopped walking and stared at him. "I hope you're joking."

"No. If Madonna wasn't already taken by a certain wiener dog I'd use that. It's a cool name."

"Lord have mercy on your future daughter, that's all I can say."

But he just laughed. "Why, what do you want to name your daughter?"

"Pearl," she said without hesitation.

"Now why does that not surprise me? You're basically my grandmother in a hot body."

Emma stared at him in astonishment. "For someone who said they wanted to get humped, you're losing that option quickly." Did he really think she wanted to be compared to his grandmother? It was one thing to tease her about liking vintage, but it was another to call her a granny. It wasn't sexy.

"What? I didn't say it was a bad thing!"

These were the moments when she realized she just did not comprehend men. At all.

KYLE WASN'T SURE why his grandmother comment had pissed Emma off so badly, given that he often teased her about her old-fashioned tastes, but she'd definitely been a little reserved since they'd walked the dogs. He had expected to get a little touchy-feeling at the ballpark, with some hand-holding, knee-rubbing, kissing action. But Emma was keeping her hands and her thoughts to herself.

So maybe calling the woman you were dating a grandma wasn't the smartest thing to do, but he hadn't meant it like that, which he had tried to explain until she had finally told him in no uncertain terms to just stop talking. Now they were sitting in the burning sun, the smell of sweaty bodies rising around them like a noxious steam, and he was not exactly enjoying himself.

"Want a hot dog?" he asked her.

"No, thanks."

She was being very polite, which was starting to piss him off. If she was mad, he wished she would just scream at him and get it over with so they could move on.

"Okay, I'll eat one for you."

"Hmm." She made a noncommittal sound, eyes trained on the field below them.

Kyle flagged down the wandering vendor and tried to fight the irritation growing inside of him. What was he supposed to do? Grovel? Screw that. He'd apologized. It wasn't exactly a heinous crime. If she was going to be that sensitive there wasn't anything he could do about it. But it was quickly becoming apparent he was wasting his Sunday.

So he did what was natural to him—he tried to joke Emma out of her mood.

"Are you sure you don't want a hot dog?" he asked, holding one tantalizingly close to her face, giving her knee a nudge with his own. "I've never known you to turn down a wiener when I was offering it."

EMMA TURNED TO LOOK at Kyle, astonished. Did he have no clue she was in a lousy mood? She did not feel like having juvenile sexual innuendos tossed her way all afternoon. But he seemed to have no idea that she was upset or why she was upset. It wasn't particularly that he had said she reminded him of his grandmother, though she wasn't exactly overjoyed with that comment. What woman wants a blue-haired granny as her point of reference?

It was more that it seemed like they always focused

on her imagined and real flaws. She was uptight. She was a granny. She wanted to be responsible instead of blowing everything off and playing around in bed all afternoon. She wanted him to go home on Sunday nights so she could sleep. She wanted to be honest instead of hiding their relationship.

It was starting to make her wonder why he even wanted to be with her at all if he thought she was that much of a drag.

"I have no interest in wiener at all this afternoon," she told him succinctly. She focused on the baseball game, even though she had no clue what was going on, given that she'd spent the past hour silently seething and she wasn't sports savvy on the best of days.

"Damn. That's brutal," he said, but he didn't sound particularly upset. He sounded like he was clowning around with his buddies. "I guess the score here really is zero. Nothing like blue balls on a Sunday afternoon."

Emma counted to three so she didn't say something she would regret. She told him quite carefully, "I am not in the mood for joking around. I can't be teased out of a mood, just so you know."

"Is that a public service announcement?"

"It's called me being honest and communicating, which is something that people who perpetually make a joke out of everything seem to have a hard time doing." God, she was sweating so much she could feel rivulets running down between her shoulder blades, adding to the fact that this afternoon was an exercise in suckiness.

Kyle adjusted his baseball hat and stared at her. "Are you purposefully trying to pick a fight with me?"

"No."

"Yes, you are. And it's starting to piss me off."

"Wow, that's quite an accomplishment, then, because nothing usually gets any reaction other than laughter from you. I feel impressed with myself." So maybe sarcasm wasn't the best way to express herself, but she figured neither was sticking her tongue out at him, which was what she really wanted to do.

"So not being moody and depressed is a character flaw? Forgive me for having my shit together."

"Or maybe you just never dig deep enough to find your shit. You hover on the surface above it." Emma wasn't exactly sallying awesome metaphors at him, but he clearly got the point she was trying to make, because he swore. Colorfully.

It occurred to her that perhaps she had gone too far. But before she could retract or clarify in a way that was slightly less confrontational, she realized the woman next to her was nudging her and saying something.

"What?" she asked her, flushed and distracted.

"Look, you and your boyfriend are on the Kiss Cam."

Emma followed the finger that was pointing to the jumbo screen on the scoreboard. Oh, my God. She and Kyle were on camera. "We're on the screen," she whispered to him faintly, suddenly and completely mortified. She looked hot, sweaty and angry, a very large, very sour Emma projecting back at her ten times her normal size. It was horrifying. It was the Worst. Thing. Ever. Kyle was looking sideways at her like she was a fly who had just landed on his lunch.

But once he realized what was happening, he did

muster a smile and a wave for the camera. "We're supposed to kiss."

"I...I..." She couldn't. They were in the middle of a stupid argument. She couldn't just shift out and give him a perky kiss for the camera. It wasn't the way she worked.

So when he moved toward her, his intention to plant one on her clear, she dodged it and backed up. The crowd gave a roar of disapproval before the camera panned away from them.

"Great. Thanks for totally making me look like an ass," he told her. "I will forever be remembered as the guy whose girlfriend wouldn't kiss him. Way to make me feel like a loser."

"Am I your girlfriend?" she asked, stunned. They had never used that word before and she needed, wanted to hear him say that yes, that was exactly how he felt about her. She realized that none of her other insecurities or fears about her personality would be valid if that's how he felt. She wouldn't have to worry he would throw her over at any given second for a woman who didn't talk like a grandmother and who didn't always want to put duty before fun.

But he didn't answer the way she wanted him to.

Clearly still angry with her, what he said was, "At the moment, I'm not too sure what you are."

It was more than she could handle. Emma stood straight up, kicking over the soft drink she'd had at her feet. She grabbed her clutch and shoved past Kyle, knocking his knees together.

"Where the hell are you going?" he asked, sounding exasperated.

Emma paused in shoving past him, her ass in his face. "Anywhere that you are not!" she snapped.

"Whatever." The word was slightly muffled by her butt, but she still heard it.

Gasping, Emma said "Excuse me" to the fans sitting next to Kyle as she squeezed past them and burst into the aisle. Jogging up the concrete steps, flushed with heat and anger, she fought the urge to break into tears. She had no idea where she was going but she had to get some air. Some space.

Her phone buzzed in her pocket. She pulled it out and saw it was a text message from her mother.

Buck's watching ball game and saw you on the kiss cam. Said you were a sourpuss. Loosen up honey. LOL.

Fabulous. Wonderful.

Even her own mother thought she was a dour old lady.

She promptly burst into tears, wanting to go home where she could cuddle with the dachshunds and drink iced tea with a tissue in her pocket like the old lady she was. She texted Kyle.

Can we leave?

No.

Really? Emma stared at her phone.

Why not?

I'm watching the game.

So much for him being the most considerate man she'd ever met.

I'm taking a cab then.

Okay. TTYL.

Talk to you later. Wow. Emma felt like she'd been punched in the ovaries.

Not a good feeling.

11

"I'm not exactly sure what happened," Kyle said, feeling more than a little bewildered as he sat on his brother's deck and watched his niece leaping around the yard in some interpretive dance that made him suspect she had to use the bathroom. "Hey, Anna, do you have to use the potty?" he called down to her, momentarily distracted.

She shook her head and Jason told him, "She always says no. Carrie thinks it's a power struggle. I just think it's because she's having too much fun to stop and take a crap. But, anyway, you were there with Emma, you have to know what happened."

"No. I really don't," he said in all honesty, taking a sip of his beer. They had steaks grilling, and under different circumstances he would be happy to be hanging out with his brother and his family. But he wasn't supposed to be crashing Jason's Sunday-night dinner, he was supposed to be with Emma. Only she had left the baseball game in a cab. A cab. Who did that?

"The day started out just fine. We walked the dogs,

the usual, though she wouldn't have sex with me before the game, now that I think about it." Kyle frowned at the memory. Did that mean something?

"Oh, gee, the problems you have." Jason rolled his eyes at him. "Has it been a while? Is the magic gone already or something? Maybe she just thinks of you as a friend."

"We did last night, and trust me, the magic is not gone." Not for him, anyway. Given Emma's four orgasms, he didn't think it was over for her, either. "I think the problem started when I was teasing her and I said she's like my grandma with a hot body."

"You said what?" Jason looked at him, lip curled back in an expression of horror.

"What?" he asked, defensively. "We're a family that likes a laugh. I mean look at your freaking shirt."

His brother was wearing a T-shirt that stated World's Hottest Dad.

"Oh, my child, you have much to learn." Jason stood up and used tongs to flip the steaks on the grill. "I hope you apologized."

"I did, but she was giving me the cold shoulder at the baseball game. I tried to flirt with her and lighten up the mood, but she wasn't having any of it. Then she refused to kiss me. It was embarrassing." It was. He wasn't a guy who got embarrassed all that easily, but it had been like asking a girl to dance in middle school and being turned down. The ultimate public diss.

"Yeah, I saw it on TV. You did look like an ass."

"Thanks. Very helpful."

Carrie came out the sliding glass door to the deck and ruffled Kyle's hair like he was five. "Why so glum?"

"He got kiss-dissed."

"Huh?"

"At the baseball game. His girl wouldn't kiss him for the Kiss Cam."

Carrie laughed. "Oh, Lord, Kyle, I wouldn't make a big deal out of that. Some girls aren't into public make-out sessions. Some girls are just more modest. No big deal."

Her words hit him like a slap in the face. Of course she was right. Emma was modest. He knew that. Had seen firsthand at the photo shoot how difficult it had been for her to strip to her panties. It had been very uncomfortable and unnatural for her. She also never walked around naked after sex. She didn't even sleep naked. Nor did she ever wear revealing clothes. She was a girl who liked to keep her sexuality private and he knew that. Respected it.

So why had it hurt his feelings so much at the baseball game?

Because he wanted her to be as crazy about him as he was about her.

"So what happened?" Jason asked him.

"We fought about it and she left and called a cab and went home."

"You didn't stop her?" Carrie asked, aghast.

"No." He suddenly felt ashamed of that fact. But he had been too angry and proud to chase after her.

"Dude." Jason shook his head. "You owe her an apology for that one. Even pissed off, you shouldn't be letting your girl go home in a cab."

He did. He knew it. "You're right. But God, she just makes me crazy. I get completely irrational around her."

Carrie and Jason exchanged a look.

"What?" he asked, irritated that they were silently communicating about him.

Carrie smiled. "It sounds like maybe you've finally met someone who has gotten over that wall you've built."

Was that it?

He suspected it was. "So what do I do?"

"Call her. Buy flowers. Grovel. Stop being a douche bag," Jason advised.

"That's helpful. Not." Kyle was about to expand on that when his cell phone rang. "Oh, hey, this is my boss. Excuse me for a second, guys." He hit the button to answer the call. "Hello?"

"Is there a particular reason you were trying to kiss Emma Hadley at the baseball game this afternoon?" Claire sounded very put out.

Oh, shit. "Yes, there is," he said, refusing to be intimidated. "It's because we were caught on the Kiss Cam." That should have been obvious enough.

"Why the hell were you at a baseball game together? Because don't think I'm going to believe that it was a coincidence that you were sitting next to each other."

"No, it wasn't. We were hanging out. We spend time together because we're dating each other." No point in denying it. The truth was clearly out there on the jumbo screen.

"I thought I said that was against office policy," she said, her voice like broken glass.

"I don't recall that being in any HR paperwork I read when I took this job, and as long as it doesn't interfere with our work, I don't see why our personal lives matter to the *Journal*."

"How would you like to move back to Sports? Or even to the front page?"

"What?" He watched Jason pulling the steaks off the grill and frowned. "Why would you offer me either of those?" It didn't make sense that if she were upset with him she would offer him a clear promotion.

"They can be yours if you agree to stop seeing Emma."

He gasped. She had genuinely shocked him. "Are you kidding me? No!" It was a clear bribe and the very thought offended him. It probably wasn't even legal. But he wasn't about to throw away a woman he cared about for a job promotion. Regardless of the fact that at the moment Emma wasn't even speaking to him. If he were a total asshole, he could keep that information from Claire and just accept the promotion, knowing he'd most likely lost Emma, anyway.

But he didn't want to concede that he had lost her. He was going to fight for Emma, and this drove that point home for him.

"Too bad. I'm giving you the promotion, anyway. You're on front page now."

"What?" he said again. He couldn't keep up with Claire. "That's crazy."

"Not at all. I'm merely creating a little distance between the two of you at work. You can handle the change in direction. Meeting tomorrow at nine, since we'll have a lot to discuss storywise for the week."

Then she hung up on him and Kyle knew that his job at the paper had just gotten a whole lot more difficult. His job winning Emma back over had gotten damn near impossible.

"Is it true?" Sandy's head popped over Emma's cubicle wall Monday morning, her expression eager and scandalized.

"Is what true?" Emma stopped typing and tried to focus on what her coworker was saying.

"That you're dating Kyle."

"Who told you that?"

"Joe. He said everyone is talking about it. That you were on the Kiss Cam at the stadium yesterday and Claire saw it."

Oh, God, that was the last thing in the world she needed to hear when she was already stressed out. "Claire watches baseball?" That actually shocked her more than the realization that they were caught. Busted. Ironically, it appeared they weren't actually dating anymore, given that she hadn't heard a word from Kyle.

"I know, weird, right? I never took her for the sports-fan type. But apparently she is. So how long have you been seeing him? Is the sex awesome?" Sandy bit her pen like she couldn't restrain herself. "Damn, I'm so jealous."

"I'm not sure we're dating," she said honestly. "We had a disagreement yesterday and I haven't heard a word from him since. I took a cab home from the game."

"Oh. Well, that sucks." Sandy pushed up her glasses. "But was the sex good?"

That was probably the only thing that could have made her laugh under the circumstances. She shook her head. "I'm not discussing that with you."

"Throw me a bone here! I'm trying to live vicariously through you and you're making it impossible."

"Sorry to disappoint."

Sandy made a clicking sound with her teeth. "Can you believe Claire gave Kyle that promotion? I thought she would be pissed about you guys dating, not doling out promotions."

All the blood drained from Emma's face and a hot, sour taste flooded her mouth. "What are you talking about?"

"You didn't know?" Sandy's astonishment turned to horror. "Shit, sorry. I assumed you knew since you and Kyle are doing the horizontal shuffle. But he got moved to the front page."

"What?" A strange buzzing sound started in her ears and for one horrifying moment Emma thought she would faint. Clinging to her cube wall, she swallowed hard, forcing the bile that had risen back down.

"Yep. Just like that." Sandy snapped her fingers. "Must be nice to be a thirty-year-old male hottie. He gets pussy and a promotion."

Kyle had gotten the coveted position at the paper she had been working her ass off for for the past three years, and she herself had been reduced to the label of pussy for him. She wasn't sure she could actually breathe. She was fairly certain she was having a seizure or an aneurysm. She wanted to start screaming, but knew if she did, she would never stop and they would cart her off to sleep in a padded room and force her to swallow little pink pills.

She wanted to throw up. And she wanted to rip Kyle's balls right off his body and throw them in the garbage disposal. How could he take a promotion and not even bother to warn her he had? She had to hear it from Sandy?

Unfortunately, the floral deliveryman chose that particular moment to approach her. "Miss Gideon?"

"What?" She whirled around, ready to tell whoever it was to piss off, in no uncertain terms, but the man was barely visible behind a gigantic bouquet of pink Old English roses. "Can I help you?" she asked.

"These are for you." He set the vase down on her desk and handed her a clipboard. "Could you sign, please?"

She blinked, staring at the roses. Who the hell had sent her roses? She snatched the card off the fronds, ignoring the man.

These are almost as beautiful as you.
Love, Kyle

Emma dropped the card on her desk like it had scalded her. Love. He used the L word. For the first time. Now? What kind of insanity was this?

Sandy almost fell over the cubicle wall straining to read the card. She did knock over a football player bobblehead that was precariously perched on the corner and it toppled onto the deliveryman's foot. "Shit. Sorry."

"Can you sign this, please?" the man asked again, shoving the electronic tablet a little farther under her nose, clearly losing patience.

Emma did an approximation of her name and mumbled, "Thanks." Then she stood, wiping her hands on her white linen trousers. "Have you seen Kyle this morning?" she asked Sandy.

"He's in Claire's office, behind closed doors. I'm sure they're discussing important news things. Like what his salary will be and how much he'll have to kiss Claire's bony ass."

Emma gave her a grimace. "Thanks. You've been very helpful this morning, Sandy."

"I try."

"That was sarcasm!" she snapped. Then she allowed herself one long, lingering inhalation of the wondrous fragrance of the roses before she snatched up the vase and marched over to Kyle's seat, which was of course vacant since he was tête-à-tête with their boss.

Without ceremony, she tipped the vase and dumped the roses, water and all, on his chair.

Let Claire fire her for it. She didn't give a shit.

She would probably regret it later.

But at the moment, she was too furious to care.

Mindful of the glass, she carefully placed the empty vase into the wastebasket next to his desk, well aware that at least four people were gawking at her. Feeling somewhat appeased, she turned and almost ran straight into Kyle's chest.

"What the hell did you do that for?" he asked, having the nerve to actually look hurt. "I thought you would love roses. They're so vintage and elegant. Totally your style."

Damn him for knowing what she liked. She felt a tiny fissure in her armor of anger. "So? That doesn't make up for the fact that you let me take a cab home yesterday!"

"You're the one who walked away from me," he pointed out. "And then basically left without saying goodbye."

He might have a slight point, but it didn't change anything. "You could have come out to talk to me."

"Honey, you were not in the mood to talk about it.

I figured we should both have a cool-down period and then maybe we could have better results."

"Which was when you were planning to tell me you got a promotion?" she said, crossing her arms over her chest. She would not be swayed by his being rational.

"I was coming to tell you that right now. As soon as my meeting with Claire was over, but clearly, someone beat me to it. I didn't anticipate the gossipers being so aggressive." He glared at the office at large.

"When did she tell you?"

"Last night. I was in shock. She didn't give me a choice, you know. She said I had to take the position. I would have told you last night, but given we were already in the middle of a disagreement, it seemed like really bad timing." Kyle touched her arm. "I know you deserve this position and I know how hard you've worked for it. I tried to say no, honestly. Claire told me I had to take it or I would be fired. She was seriously mad about us dating, but I told her straight up I wasn't going to break up with you to save my job." He was speaking in a low voice so they wouldn't be overheard, and he had moved closer into her personal space.

It was distracting to feel his body brushing against hers, to smell the scent of him that she knew so well now. Her lips ached with the desire to feel his mouth on hers in a kiss.

Emma tried to puzzle out the logic of all he was saying. "So then why would Claire promote you after threatening to fire you?"

"She wants to split us up, clearly. My guess is she figures if she gives me your dream job, we'll fight so much that we'll be done." He gently rubbed his thumb across the bare flesh of her arm. "We won't let her do that, will we?"

"I...I don't know. I mean, no. Of course not." Emma felt the familiar ache of desire pooling between her thighs. She was a couple orgasms shy for the weekend given their fight and she was feeling it now. That had to be the only explanation for why she was suddenly tight and wet and aroused at ten in the morning at the office. "Why were we fighting again? Remind me?"

"I have no idea. I think maybe it had something to do with me being insensitive. And not respecting that you don't like to be teased, especially when you're already mad." He gave her a sweet, lopsided smile. "Lesson learned. I won't repeat that mistake."

"I was feeling insecure," she blurted out. "I wasn't sure how you feel about me."

Kyle looked astonished. "Emma." He pointed to the pile of roses on his chair. "That's how I feel about you. Well, if those roses were still in a vase."

She flushed. "Sorry about that. I was a little upset."

"I see that." He bent over and retrieved the vase, then put the roses back in it. "But I think they're salvageable. The question is, are we salvageable?"

Despite knowing it was going to drive her absolutely insane that Kyle was covering hard news, Emma couldn't resist the idea of them as a couple. She just enjoyed his company too much. Biting her lip, she nodded. "I think so."

He gave a heartfelt sigh that just melted her insides. "Good. When we're out of this damn office, I'm going to kiss the stuffing out of you."

Her lips twitched up into a smile. "Sounds messy."

Kyle laughed. "Get back to work, you sassy girl. And take your roses with you."

Emma did just that, clutching the vase to her chest like it was a trophy. In a way she supposed it was. She had just won out over her fears and Claire's meddling, and she felt pretty damn triumphant.

12

KYLE CALLED EMMA around seven, when he knew she'd be home from work and done with the salad she liked to whip together for a quick dinner. She would have pulled her blouse from her narrow skirt and let her hair down out of its tight ponytail. Maybe she would have a glass of wine in her hand. But she would have put work behind her for the day and she would be relaxed. His Emma. The one he got to experience in private, not the successful career woman everyone else in the office saw every day. Though that one was pretty damn sexy in her own right, because she was strong and competent and he found that very appealing, she didn't like to be touched. This Emma liked his hands on her, and he appreciated that very much.

"Hello?"

Kyle hit the button to turn off the radio in his car. "It's me. How are you?"

"Good. Just relaxing before I go to that film premiere at nine."

Shit. He'd forgotten about the premiere. He w̶a̶s̶ obligated to go, but Emma was. She didn't d̶ views, but she had to write up the opening of a run of six independent art films at the museum.

"I was hoping I could see you for a few minutes before you have to leave."

"I only have an hour, so there's not much time to spare."

"Well, I guess it's a good thing I'm in the parking lot of your building, then." Kyle smiled as she made an exclamation of surprise.

"What? Really?"

"Yep. I figured if you weren't home or you were busy, I was only out ten minutes. It was worth the risk if I could see you at all."

"I would love to see you," she said. "Come on up."

Her voice was soft and tender in a way that made him feel like something had shifted irrevocably inside him. "Okay, see you in a minute."

But Kyle sat in his car for a second or two, staring at his cell phone and pondering the pain he'd felt when he thought he had lost Emma, and the contentment he felt now knowing they were going to be together, after all.

Was this love?

He wasn't exactly sure. But he thought it was getting pretty damn close.

So he'd better get the hell inside before he lost more of the precious time he had.

Emma opened the door, looking exactly how he'd pictured her, hair loose, blouse untucked and slightly rumpled, feet bare. Only she also happened to be licking a frozen fruit bar. "Hi." Her tongue peeked out and slid along the rich red of the fruit bar until she reached the end, where she pulled off with a small sucking sound.

He felt his dick harden. He couldn't have asked for a better presentation. Her lips were swollen and moist and tinted a deep blush from the fruit. He wasn't sure if it was strawberry or raspberry. Only one way to find out. "Can I have a bite?"

"Sure." She tilted the stick so the bar angled toward him.

But he ignored the offer and instead placed his lips on her, tasting the sweetness, his tongue plunging inside her mouth to taste what she had to offer, a tangy fruity delight. When he was done kissing her, he bit the plumpness of her bottom lip.

"Mmm. Strawberry." He then went ahead and bit the frozen treat itself.

Emma's eyes had darkened and she looked languid and relaxed. Ready for some makeup sex. "Is that your favorite?"

"You're my favorite."

She smiled and closed the door behind him. "You have about forty minutes, that's it. Especially if I'm going to need a shower afterward."

He tried to put on a face of mock innocence. "I have no idea what you're talking about. I just came here to sit on the couch and hold your hand and talk. I don't know why that would result in you having to take a shower."

"Is that why you're already pulling your tie off?"

Busted. "I'm relaxing." He kicked off his shoes and started unbuttoning his dress shirt.

"Let me help you relax." Emma yanked the bottom of his shirt from his pants and pulled his belt open. Then she efficiently unzipped her skirt and let it fall to the floor.

Oh, yeah. He loved her. She was a woman who got things done and he so very much appreciated that.

Another thirty seconds and she had her blouse and bra off. Just bam. She was almost completely naked, her perfect breasts bared, rosy nipples tight and practically begging him to suck them. Then her panties were gone like they'd never been there at all, and he was staring at the apex of her thighs. A small ribbon of blond hair coyly hiding her sex from him.

"You're overdressed," she told him. She glanced at the wall clock. "And you're down to thirty-seven minutes. You'd better get in the bedroom." She licked her fruit bar.

Kyle groaned.

How was a man expected to be anything but hard 24/7 with a woman like that?

"Want some more?" Emma held it out teasingly. Then she let it slip and swipe across her nipple. "Oops. I got some on me."

Oh, someone was in a mood that he really, really liked. "Oh, no, that's terrible. Let me see if I can help."

Kyle stripped his shirt off then yanked his undershirt over his head and let them drop to the floor next to her clothes. He inched down his zipper as he bent over Emma and flicked his tongue across her nipple, appreciating both the tangy burst of sweetness from the melted treat, and the sigh of delight she gave.

"Did I get it all?" he asked as he shoved his pants down his thighs and stepped out of them.

"You might have missed a spot," she said with a sly grin, causing his balls to shrink up tightly and his cock to throb.

This definitely wasn't a side of Emma just anyone

got to see. Kyle was really damn grateful she chose to share it with him.

"Oh, yeah?" Kyle took the fruit bar from her and trailed it all the way down her abdomen right to that little patch of hair above her clitoris. She gasped from the cold. He bit another piece off the bar and moved it around in his mouth before covering her nipple again.

She made a growling sound in the back of her throat that he'd never heard before.

He sucked the tight bud, the chunk of icy sweetness resting right on top of her nipple, sliding over her flesh as he pulled her in and out of his mouth. Her fingers dug into his waist and her head fell back while her hips started to rock forward, desperate for the attention of his hard cock.

Straining the limits of his briefs, he let her bump their bodies together in a teasing mock sex while he swallowed the mostly melted bite and took the tip of his tongue down the curve of her breast, along her rib cage.

"We're going to run out of time," she moaned, sounding desperate. "You'd better put it in."

"Shh."

"Don't shush me," she snapped.

Kyle grinned against her stomach as he moved lower. When he dipped his finger inside her moistness, her irritation morphed into a moan of pleasure. He brought his finger to his mouth and tasted it. "Sweet."

To his surprise, Emma took matters into her own hand. Breathing hard, she just turned on her heel and walked down the hall to her bedroom, her heart-shaped ass swinging enticingly in front of him. Taking another bite of the bar, he chewed it loudly and ambled off after her. He wanted to see what she would do while waiting for him. Pausing to take another bite, he leaned casually on the door frame and watched her climb onto the bed on all fours.

For a second, he thought he wasn't going to be able to stop himself from striding over there and just shoving himself inside her at that blatant invitation, but he restrained himself. Crossing his ankles, he kept his briefs on as further torment and just continued to lick the remains of the fruit bar.

"What are you doing?" she asked impatiently over her shoulder, her backside wiggling alluringly.

"Finishing this. It's good."

Her expression was incredulous. Shifting onto her side, she toyed with her nipple and restlessly shifted her ankles. "Come here and let me have another bite."

She was attempting to seduce him over to the bed, and there was no doubt it was working. Kyle held the fruit bar in his mouth with his lips to free his hands and shucked his briefs, before heading over to her without hesitation, a dog racing for a treat.

Ignoring the erection that was damn near in danger of taking out her eye, she pulled the stick out of his mouth. When she licked and sucked the bar, she also got his finger, drawing them both between her lips into the moist heat. And with that, he was done playing around. She had turned his teasing game right around on him, and his restraint shattered.

They were down to maybe thirty minutes, but he figured this was only going to take five.

Yanking the stick out of her hand, he tossed it into the wastebasket next to her nightstand and pulled open the drawer, where they had started stocking condoms. While he worked on that with one hand, he worked on

Emma with the other. She was still lounging on her side, and it was easy enough to slip his fingers between her legs and stroke her into the sounds of ecstasy he loved to hear from her mouth.

"You like that?"

She nodded.

"Want more?"

"Yes."

He was beyond happy to give it to her. He knew she expected him to thrust inside her, but he dipped his head down instead and used his tongue to catapult her into a quick, tight orgasm. He loved when she came for him, loved the way her body tensed around him. There was nothing more satisfying than knowing he had brought her that kind of pleasure, that his touch could trip off such intensity of physical sensation in her that her eyes drifted closed and her moans escaped without control.

Only when she was coming back down to earth, relaxing her back down into the mattress and reaching for him in silent plea and invitation, did Kyle move his cock between her thighs and give her what they both wanted. As he sank into her wondrous heat, Kyle met her glassy gaze and said without forethought, without warning, without any care for the consequences, "I love you."

He wasn't sure who was more surprised, him or her. Her eyes widened and a soft sigh left her mouth. Feeling more expectant than he would have thought, he pushed in and out, slowly, bringing them together in the most intimate way possible, while feeling completely at ease with what he had told her, whether he had realized those words would appear or not. He did love her. It was simple, uncomplicated, just there and right and true. She was genuine, caring and loyal, and he loved her.

It would be amazing if she responded in kind, but if she didn't, he was okay with that. He'd get her eventually.

But she looked up at him, her expression serious yet vulnerable. "I love you, too."

That's all it took. His heart swelling, Kyle looped his fingers through hers, held on, and plummeted over the edge of desire. As he came deep inside her, he felt more connected to Emma than to any other woman he'd ever met. It didn't necessarily make sense, but it was there, and it had been from the beginning, that undeniable spark, which had grown into a full five-alarm fire of passion and love.

It was good to know he wasn't burning alone.

As his orgasm faded, he leaned down and kissed her hard, feeling that would better express emotion than words. He flopped beside her and listened to the sound of her breathing slow to a more natural rate.

"I have a confession to make," Emma told him a minute or two later as they lay entwined on her bed, a tangled mass of warm bodies.

Not words any man wants to hear. Had she hooked up with someone in the twenty hours they'd been broken up? No, that was definitely not Emma's style. He didn't think she was going to announce she had no intention of dating him anymore, either, given she had just said she loved him, yet a prickle of fear still raced up his spine.

So he reacted in the way that was natural for him. "Well, it can't be that you have a third nipple," he joked.

She rolled her eyes predictably. "That definitely would have been a challenge to hide for the last month."

"What is it then?" He knew better than to throw out another ridiculous suggestion. It would just irritate her. One time was cute. A second time, he was pushing his luck.

So he just waited. Nothing was going to ruin this moment. He wouldn't let it.

EMMA WASN'T EVEN certain why she had chosen this particular time to bring up the subject. Maybe it was pure wimpiness on her part given she had to leave in less than ten minutes, so there wouldn't be much time to really discuss it. Or maybe it was because she felt close to him right then, curled up in bed, physically and emotionally satisfied with their relationship. He had told her that he loved her. Granted, it was whispered in the middle of sex, so it wasn't entirely reliable, but it had still felt amazing to hear those words coming from his lips. Directed at her.

The last of her insecurities had evaporated entirely.

So she needed to be entirely truthful with him, because whether he had meant it or not, she certainly had. She did love Kyle. It was strange and wondrous to contemplate, but it was true. She had been drawn to him from day one, and by the time he had so readily agreed to walk her mom's short-legged dogs, she had been head over heels. There hadn't really been any preventing it.

"I found out who Ian Bainbridge's stalker is," she told him sheepishly, not entirely sure why she had kept her research activities a secret from him. But maybe she hadn't wanted him to talk her out of it, or tell her she was nuts for risking her job.

"What?" He just looked at her blankly. "What do you mean? How did you do that?"

"Well, like we talked about before, Ian said the stalker was signing her emails 'Savannah,' and according to her, he used to frequent a pub in Pittsburgh where she worked. Ian doesn't remember meeting her, though. I made a few phone calls, because how many Savannahs can there be, and I'm sure she's the right one. I found out she was in the appropriate cities at the right times for the various shoots."

"How did you do that?"

"You don't want to know." It might have involved posing as Savannah herself to the cell-phone company, but she didn't feel he needed to know that.

Kyle still looked sleepy and sex-rumpled. He just raised an eyebrow. "What are you planning to do with this information?"

"I don't know. I was thinking of going to the police. Or contacting her."

"No, don't contact her. That's insane. She's not going to tell you anything and she's clearly crazy."

"Well, I can't tell Ian. I mean, what if he does something vigilante-like?" That did worry her. Ian seemed like a very nonchalant and stable guy, but she didn't know him, and handing over someone's identity seemed like it had the potential for an ugly confrontation.

"You should tell the police what you know, then drop it. It's out of your hands at that point."

"You think so?" Emma knew he was right, but it didn't sit well with her. "I guess you're right."

"You know I am." He kissed her forehead. "Now stop worrying and get your sweet ass dressed. You have a film premiere to go to." He lightly smacked her backside.

Part of her still harbored delusions that if she just hit on the right story, Claire would see her value and promote her. But she had a feeling that was just wishful thinking. If she wanted Claire to respect her, she had to grow a penis.

Not happening.

Emma put aside thoughts of stalkers, eccentric photographers and biased bosses and concentrated on the man in front of her. "Thanks for stopping by."

"My pleasure." He peeled himself off the mattress. "Damn, I don't want you to go. I don't want to go home. I want to stay here for about a year."

"Somebody's got to pay the rent," she told him, sitting up herself and pondering what she should wear.

"Stop making sense. Just let me pretend for a minute."

Like she was going to pretend it didn't bother her that he was going to be covering real news stories instead of human-interest pieces? She shoved that thought aside and gave him a smile. "Sorry. But instead of pretending, how about you come to the premiere with me? Then we can get naked again. Rinse and repeat."

Kyle paused in pulling on his briefs. "You are brilliant, Emma. Absolutely brilliant. If it's not a secret at work anymore, who cares about being seen together?"

"I don't think we were really all that concerned about it before, to tell you the truth," she said. "We did end up on TV at a baseball game."

"True. But we didn't seek that out."

"Nor did we exactly stay hidden." Emma grabbed a pair of panties and a bra from her dresser and headed to take the quickest shower ever known to man. Or more accurately, to woman.

It was going to be smooth sailing from here on out. No work drama. Personal bliss.

What could possibly go wrong?

13

As IT TURNED OUT, a lot could go wrong. In very quick succession, the course of Emma's week changed from a honeymoon of sorts to a feeling more appropriate for a funeral. By Friday she wanted to throw herself down in the dirt on the grave of her career and pound her fists while screaming, "Why? Why, why, why?"

First off, at their Monday planning meeting, Claire had dumped the type of busywork assignments on her that Emma hated, from writing copy for the opening of a new art supply store, to attending a hospital benefit with a huge splashy write-up that had to be as large as the full page ad the hospital had taken to run alongside it. Both were the type of advertising disguised as news stories Emma hated to write, and Claire knew that. Claire also knew Emma was not a gofer, yet for some reason she had elected Emma to do a Tuesday coffee run and to supply Claire with a ride home from work Wednesday since her car was in the shop.

The culmination of a lousy workweek was her annual employee review on Friday.

The minute Emma stepped into Claire's office, she knew it wasn't going to go well.

"You know that personally I like you, Emma," was how Claire started the review.

Actually, she didn't. Emma forced herself to sit still in the chair opposite Claire's desk and not fidget in nervousness. "Thank you."

"But we have, of course, had our differences of opinion when it comes to the quality of your work. Sometimes you lose focus on the aim of Life & Style. As I'm sure you know, these are dicey days for dailies. Circulation is down. Advertising is down. Costs are up."

Oh, no. Oh, no, no, no. This sounded like a review that was about to turn into a pink slip. Emma's palms went clammy and she broke out into a sweat. She nodded, her earrings bobbing, because she had no idea what to actually say.

"All departments have been forced to make some drastic cuts and I'm sorry to say we need to eliminate a position, and that it's going to have to be yours."

There it was. The ax hitting the chopping block. All her hard work, all her devotion dismissed. Poof. Gone. Just like that. "I don't understand. You moved Kyle to the front page. Who is going to cover Life & Style? You'll be severely understaffed."

Claire just shrugged. "We'll have to do some shuffling. It's going to be hell for the rest of us, believe me. We're all getting a raw deal here, Emma."

Uh. Emma thought she was the one getting the rawest deal of all since she was the one being fired. "I've been here for three years," she said, because she couldn't just stand up and walk out without at least an attempt at trying to keep her job. "Isn't there someone else with less seniority?"

Claire's lips pursed. "You were on probation for the incident with the Ian Bainbridge story. Then there were rumors about you disrupting the workplace by throwing a vase of flowers at another staff member."

"What?" Emma sputtered. "I did not throw a vase of flowers!" Okay, so she had dumped them on Kyle's chair, but she wouldn't exactly call that a workplace disruption. It had been done and over in three minutes. But she did feel her cheeks flush. The bottom line was, it hadn't been professional and she knew that.

"I didn't really have a choice when it came down to it. How could I let someone with a spotless record go when yours is not?" If Claire smiled a little like the cat that had gotten the cream, Emma couldn't exactly argue, could she?

The witch had found a perfect way to get rid of her without raising any eyebrows. If it wasn't her behind in a sling, Emma would almost be impressed with the maneuvering of her suddenly former boss. Since she was the one losing her livelihood, she couldn't bring herself to do much more than nod and stand abruptly.

"When is this effective?"

"Immediately."

"As in, today?" Emma gawked at her.

Claire tried to look contrite, but she didn't quite pull it off. "I'm sorry, Emma. You'll be entitled to your vacation and personal days, of course."

That was a small consolation.

Stunned, Emma wandered out of Claire's office, wishing that today of all days was not when Kyle had left work early to go see his new baby niece for a couple of hours. She really needed someone to look her in the eye and keep her from bursting into tears in front of the entire staff.

Fortunately, no one was paying attention to her. They were all busy clearing their desks to cut out of the office for the weekend. She made it to her cubicle without having to speak to anyone and sank into her chair, her hands shaking. What was she going to do?

After swallowing hard for a minute or two, she realized pragmatically, the only thing she could do was clear off her desk, cancel her corporate email and go home. It was a horrifying and ignominious ending to her career at the paper, collecting her personal mementoes and slinking out. It did not do good things for her self-esteem.

Neither did Ian Bainbridge's stalker calling her a fat cow.

Glancing through her email, Emma gave a start, her heart pounding, when she saw she'd received a response from Savannah in her email. Earlier in the week, she had sent a message to one of the contact addresses she had unearthed for Savannah and had inquired about her interactions with Ian Bainbridge, trying to be friendly and nonthreatening, pointing out her own participation in the shoot and her article.

Savannah's response read, "I searched you. Nice hair. Stay away from Ian, you fat cow."

Just not helpful at the moment.

Granted, she should not take the insults of a deluded stalker personally, but it was a little difficult to swallow the double whammy of having both her hair and her weight called into question. She was a woman, after all. Those were vulnerable spots.

On top of being fired? Not a fun Friday, that was for sure.

But it was safe to say she would have overlooked all of that if Savannah hadn't taken it one step further by writing a scathing follow-up email to Emma, calling into question her ethics as a journalist by attaching an extremely zoomed-in close-up of Emma at the shoot, with terrified eyes and breasts peeking out of the sides of her forearms. Along with that was a picture of Emma and Ian bent over talking at the bar the night after the shoot, and Savannah's implications that naked sluts who drank with photographers got their jobs the old-fashioned way. Savannah had threatened to post it all online in a blog.

It was just a stupid little threat, because any blog would be hidden in the flotsam of the internet, but there was still a possibility that if someone searched her name, they would discover it. Emma could not under any circumstances have anyone reading that garbage if she ever wanted to be hired full-time in news again. Or have them seeing that blown-up picture of her. She would never be taken seriously ever again, and she would be inundated with specials on gym memberships from local fitness centers. Neither of which she wanted to endure.

Who knew if Savannah would carry out her threat, but since her elevator didn't seem to go to the top floor, Emma thought the odds were fairly high.

Darting her eyes around the office every ten seconds, afraid someone would see the pictures she was looking at, Emma debated whether or not she should just delete the emails or if she should respond.

But if Savannah had a picture of Emma and Ian at

the bar talking, that meant she was following him and secretly photographing him, which was beyond creepy. It also meant that Emma herself was now on Savannah's radar and was potentially a target.

Before she could stop herself, she had typed, "Let's talk about this. I want to hear your side of the story," and hit Send.

Wasn't that what all stalkers wanted, to have their nutty point of view heard?

There wasn't even time to debate the wisdom of a dialogue with a lunatic when Savannah responded. "Why would I want to talk to you?"

Emma bit her lip. This would be her only chance to get the story. While it wouldn't get her a job back, it would give her great satisfaction to turn the information over to the police. Maybe it would be a positive mark on her resume instead of a blotch.

Or maybe it was just the worst idea ever. But while she was debating, Savannah emailed her again. "Plaid Kilt in Pittsburgh, tonight at 7:00. Parking lot. Be there. Unless you're too busy being a slut to meet me."

Heart thumping at an unnaturally high rate, Emma didn't hesitate. "See you then."

What was with the slurs on her character lately? First Rosanna going for the jugular in the bar, and now this unknown stalker? Emma wasn't used to it, and she had to admit, it got her fired up in indignation. She was a businesswoman. She was highly professional. She was...unemployed.

Good grief. Gathering her things as rapidly as possible, Emma deleted her work account after forwarding the emails from Savannah to her private email. Feeling nauseous, she hightailed it out of the office she had devoted the majority of her waking hours to for almost three years, unable to even say goodbye to her coworkers.

It felt like she was either going to need about six pints of ice cream or three bottles of wine, neither of which would be healthy.

Avoiding both of those was the only way she could explain how she wound up Friday night lying to all and sundry and driving to Pittsburgh to meet a crazy woman in a dark parking lot.

When Kyle called her to ask what her plans were for the night, she lied with an ease she hadn't known she was capable of. "I'm going to the movies with my cousin. How was the baby?"

"Pink. Round. You know, like babies are. But she's very cute and very solemn. She had kind of a Gandhi stare going on. I feel wiser just from holding her."

Emma forced a laugh. "That's awesome. You're still hanging out with your brother and your friends tonight, right?"

"Yep. See you tomorrow, babe."

She hung up after responding, bile in her throat. She should have at least told him about her job, but she couldn't make the words leave her mouth. It was so embarrassing. It was like everything she had devoted herself to had been a joke. That she was a joke. The economy wasn't her fault and she knew it, but it was very difficult not to take being laid off personally.

It was better to just meet Savannah and then spend the night processing what had happened while eating chocolate ice cream, wearing enormous pajama pants and watching mind-numbing sitcoms. Tomorrow she would tell Kyle. She did dial Sandy as she drove down the Pennsylvania Turnpike because it occurred to her that someone should know where she was in case she got into trouble, such as death or jail, and while Sandy would enjoy being in the know, she wouldn't be concerned enough to try to talk Emma out of it. That was the theory, anyway, and Sandy didn't let her down.

"You're insane," Sandy said when Emma told her what she was doing.

"Probably." Hell, she couldn't argue that.

"This isn't going to make Claire give you your old job back, you know."

Ugh. Word traveled fast.

"I know." Claire, aka The Helmet-Haired Undersexed Bitch From Hell. Not that Emma was holding a grudge or anything. "How did you know I got fired?"

"Technically you were laid off, not fired. And Claire sent out a memo. It included stats about productivity and how staff reshuffling will commence immediately. Blah, blah. Basically it was to tell us all that we have to do more work, when we're already doing the work of two people. You're lucky you got out when you did."

"Except I have no job!"

Which had led to the course she was currently on, barreling down the highway for what was probably a complete waste of gas, time and the remaining shreds of her credibility and sanity.

"Good point."

"Maybe I should turn around." Emma cranked the air-conditioning up one more notch and switched lanes to pass a semitruck hauling hundreds of chickens. Ironic. "No. Scratch that. No, I'm not turning around. I'm doing this to prove a point to myself and to Claire. That I was right all along."

"Right about what?"

"That Savannah has the potential to be dangerous."

"How are you going to prove that? By having her attack you? Yep, that will prove it all right." Sandy made a rustling sound then yelled, "Knock it off! God, I get so tired of the grandkids having their burping contests. It ruins my Friday-night mood, especially considering my husband usually enters as a walk-on contestant and wins."

Emma wanted to laugh, because Sandy did crack her up, but she was too nervous to do much more than cough. "Are you going to be around all night? Will you pick up if I call? You know, in case I need help."

"Of course. But I'm not sure what you think I can do to help you sitting in the suburbs of Cleveland when you're diving into the underbelly of Pittsburgh."

"Pittsburgh has an underbelly?"

"Everywhere has an underbelly. Even Wisconsin has an underbelly."

"Okay, well, thanks. And just call the police or whatever. But nothing is going to happen. I might get lost but that's the worst that can happen, right?"

Sandy made a noncommittal sound in Emma's ear. "What did you tell Kyle?"

"That I'm at the movies with my cousin."

"He bought that?"

"I'm not known to lie, so yes, I think he believed me." She felt terrible about it, in fact. But she had known what Kyle would say—that she was insane. Only he would put a lot more emotion into the statement than Sandy had. Most likely, he would sit on her to keep her home, or even worse, distract her with multiple orgasms until she forgot what she was supposed to be doing. He'd play dirty pool and she couldn't risk that.

He still had his job. There was no way she could logically explain to him why she needed to do this, even if it was stupid and potentially dangerous. He hadn't been called a fat cow.

"So what exactly are you hoping to accomplish?" Sandy asked.

"I want her to confess to any or all of her activities. At the very least, I want her to say something threatening, either to me or in regards to Ian." Emma checked her GPS for the seventeenth time and cleared her throat. Saying her intention out loud made it sound even stupider than she thought it was. "Okay, I need to concentrate on these directions so I'll call you later."

"Good luck."

Emma could practically hear Sandy's head shaking back and forth. "You're going to need it," she added.

"I've got this," Emma told her. She hoped.

"She what?" Kyle stopped walking so suddenly his brother Jason ran straight into his back. "Are you freaking kidding me?"

"Hey," Jason said in irritation, but Kyle barely heard him.

The world came to a screeching halt as he tried to process the words Sandy was saying to him on his cell phone.

"Of course I'm serious. Emma is on her way to Pittsburgh right now to meet up with that stalker, and I think you need to stop her. She may be a crack reporter, and a smart girl, but streetwise she is not. She's walking into a disaster, in my opinion."

"Oh, my God." Kyle swore. And then he swore again. "What was she thinking?"

"I think she was thinking she could get her job back."

And then Sandy filled him in on how Claire had laid Emma off. He couldn't believe it.

He should have known better. He should have realized that Emma was too torn apart about Claire's little announcement to just blithely go to the movies with a cousin she'd never mentioned before. Emma was devastated about the whole work situation, and Kyle knew she probably wasn't sharing her feelings wholly with him on the subject because he had gotten a promotion while she'd gotten the shaft. Kicking himself for swallowing her line that she was okay, he felt waves of guilt and fear toss over him. He wanted to yell. "Tracking down some crazy chick and questioning her is going to result in her getting a shiv in her gut, not her job back. I'm going after her. Where is she?" Kyle's mind was already racing ahead. Emma had an hour lead on him, which was a very dangerous gap. Anything could happen before he got there.

"At some bar named the Plaid Kilt."

"Okay, I'll find her. I'm so glad you emailed me."

He had been on his way to beer and wings with the guys when he had gotten an urgent email on his phone from Sandy saying she didn't know his cell number, but that she was worried about Emma. Sandy wasn't known to overreact, so he had emailed her back with his number, his heart leaping out of his chest with concern. Fortunately, she had been checking her email and called him right away with her information that Emma was potentially driving into danger.

"Please knock some sense into her. She may be a bit of a priss, but I happen to really like her and I don't want anything happening to her."

"I happen to really like her, too." Kyle tapped Jason on the shoulder and made a gesture to wait as his group of three friends was about to go into the restaurant. "Don't worry, I'm going to bring her back intact."

So that he could kill her for taking such a huge risk.

EMMA WAS RUNNING late for her scheduled meeting with Savannah. She had gotten off the turnpike to get gas and had become snarled in a traffic jam swirling around a stalled pickup truck. By the time she filled her tank, used the restroom, bought a much-needed soft drink and got back on the road, she'd lost thirty minutes.

Concerned that Savannah wouldn't wait for her, she scanned the street for the parking lot behind the bar.

Tucking her cell phone into her pocket, Emma made sure it would be ready to start recording as soon as she stepped out of the car. She wore a skirt, heels and a blazer, because she wanted to appear professional. Noticing the gravel parking lot and shadowy corners behind the bar, she was regretting that choice. Feeling like she'd fallen into a Robert De Niro movie, Emma lamented her squeaky-clean past. If she had done drugs or dated a mafia man, she would be better equipped to handle a situation like this. As it stood, she felt a bit like an Ewok going up against a Stormtrooper. It wasn't going to be a fair fight, but she could only hope that she would appear unthreatening to Savannah.

But she had underestimated the stalker.

A woman moved out of the shadows behind the

Dumpster the minute Emma parked her car and got out, her cell phone recording.

"Over here," the woman said, jerking her head in the opposite direction of Emma's car.

Great. Reluctantly, she followed her. Savannah stopped by a rusted metal door that went into the back of the bar presumably, and turned to face her. "You don't look nearly as fat in person as you do in pictures," she said.

Really? Emma tried not to feel annoyed and failed miserably. "Well, yeah, they say the camera adds ten pounds, but you don't have to be a bitch about it." Enough was enough.

Savannah was thin, of course, but she was actually very plain. She wore nerd glasses. She had a pale long face, thin lips and thick eyebrows. Her hair was a nondescript brown, and she was swimming in her boyfriend jeans, dirty oxfords on her feet. She wore an army jacket over a T-shirt, and every one of her fingers was covered in pewter rings of various shapes and sizes, most overwhelming her delicate hands.

The weird thing was, she reminded Emma of someone; she just couldn't place who. Putting her hands in the pockets of her blazer, she hoped like hell the phone was recording correctly.

The girl laughed. "I like you more already. So what's the deal here? What are you offering me exactly and what do you want in return?"

"I'll write your story if you promise not to post that story to your blog." She wasn't about to tell Savannah she no longer had a job.

"That's it? That's all you want?" Savannah looked unimpressed.

"I want the full truth. I want to know exactly how you've managed to follow Ian Bainbridge's every move. I want to know your ultimate goal."

"Those things are easy enough. I want to marry Ian. He's my soul mate."

Just a smidge of crazy had crept into her tone, and it made Emma shiver in the dark. "So you have a plan to get his attention?"

"Yes. It also involves eliminating the competition. Which includes you, sweetie."

That was a little unnerving. Starting to feel alarmed, Emma glanced around. The parking lot was empty and she was fifty feet from her car. "I'm not competition. I have no interest in Ian. I have a boyfriend." Who was going to dump her once he realized she had lied to him. Why the hell had she thought this was a good idea?

"I saw you slutting up to Ian at the bar that night. You totally want in his pants and I'm not going to let you get away with interfering in my relationship with him."

What relationship? As far as Emma could tell, there wasn't one, which made this whole conversation super weird. She was starting to realize that there was no reasoning with a lunatic.

"What are you going to do?" Emma scoffed, hoping she sounded confident, and not about to pee her pencil skirt, which was how she really felt.

Savannah laughed, and again the feeling that Emma knew her nagged at her. That voice was familiar. "If you don't back down, I'll destroy your career."

That actually made Emma feel a little less afraid. She gave a short laugh. "My career is already in the toilet, honey. Hit me with your best shot."

"How about this picture sent to your boss? Or taken out as an ad in your paper? Or spam emailed to one million social network users?" Savannah held out her cell phone and Emma leaned forward to see what it was.

"What is it? I can't see anything."

"It's a picture of you doing some very, very naughty things."

For a second, cold fear gripped her. But then she relaxed. She hadn't done anything untoward. The only man she had been involved with in a millennium was Kyle, and they had never fooled around in public, so there was no way Savannah could have the goods on her. "I don't believe you."

"Are you willing to take that chance? Or maybe you don't care if the world knows how much you like doggie style."

Damn, the bitch was good. She had Emma doubting herself. She was 99 percent sure Savannah was bluffing, but what if she wasn't? A lot of women probably enjoyed sex on all fours, so that didn't prove anything other than that she had guessed correctly, but the thought of the world having access to naked pictures of her during sex was horrifying. Once they were out there, there was really no way to ever completely get rid of it.

The thought was mind-numbing.

"Or maybe you'd like to see the video of your boyfriend with my sister? Given what I've seen of him with both you and her, he does like oral sex."

Oh, no, she didn't. The blood leeched from Emma's face and she flexed her fingers, which had suddenly gone numb. "Your sister?" she asked, hoarsely.

"Yes. She doesn't mind that she's getting your sloppy seconds, but I don't think that's your style. You don't know Kyle is screwing around, do you?"

It all came crashing over her then who Savannah reminded her of.

Rosanna.

Ian's assistant.

Savannah's sister.

That was how Savannah knew where he was when, what hotels he was in, the details of his shoot. His assistant had access to all that information and she was feeding it straight to his stalker.

While Savannah didn't necessarily look like Rosanna, she had the same timbre to her voice and she shared a nose and jawline. But more than that, it was something about her arrogance, her willingness to just slice and dice with words so casually, that had niggled at the back of Emma's subconscious.

"Kyle is not screwing around with Rosanna." The protest sounded weak even to her own ears. She knew it wasn't true. She knew Kyle wouldn't say he loved her while he fooled around on her. She knew that.

For the most part.

But now that the image of Kyle between Rosanna's thighs had been thrust into her mind by Savannah's mean-spirited suggestion, she couldn't get rid of it. It made her focus sluggish and she frowned, determined to redirect the conversation. "So your sister did your spying for you? She told you where the photo shoots were going to be and how to avoid security?"

"You're not as dumb as you look. Though it took you about a thousand years and me telling it to you to figure it out." Savannah rolled her eyes behind her glasses.

"So what is your plan now? Why do you disrupt Ian's shoots? I mean, don't you think that you're just making him angry? Wouldn't he be more likely to fall in love with you if you weren't destroying his career?" That truly baffled Emma and she figured she might as well ask the obvious.

"I do it because I can't have all these naked tramps around him. He needs to stop with the disgusting nude photography." Savannah's voice had gone from controlled boredom to agitation.

Emma knew the key to a good interview was to get your subject to confess something they hadn't intended to reveal. So feeling like she was on the verge of pushing Savannah to that point, she said, "Doesn't it bother you that your sister gets to spend so much time with Ian and you don't?" It was a gamble, but it was a good hit. Savannah frowned, her grip tightening on her cell phone.

"No. I mean, a little. I mean, it's necessary. Rosanna is a slut, so she's perfectly happy to sleep with guys who participate in the shoots. But she wouldn't with Ian, of course. She knows that he's mine." But she suddenly looked unsure of herself for the first time. "Why, do you know something?"

"No. It just seems risky to me, that's all. If Rosanna likes men, plural, in large quantities, it seems like it might be tempting. It would certainly be convenient."

Savannah pushed up her glasses. "You're messing with my head."

Bingo.

Emma figured that made two of them. They were in a stalemate, staring at each other for a good sixty seconds.

When Savannah suddenly lunged at her, she was caught off guard.

But Emma did manage to take off running across the gravel parking lot in the dark, cursing the decision to wear strappy heels.

14

KYLE WAS SWEATING and swearing by the time he found the bar and drove around behind it, searching for the parking lot and Emma. He had driven to Pittsburgh with a blatant disregard for the speed limit and his personal safety. He had tried to call Emma a dozen times easily, but she hadn't answered. He called Sandy back and asked her to try and she was unsuccessful, as well.

It made his heart crawl so far up his throat, he was going to be forced to eat it to get it back down.

He was going to have a serious discussion with Emma and extract a promise that she would never do this to him again. Better yet, he would make love to her so thoroughly, she would agree to anything he suggested.

Every possible horror scenario he could think of had rolled through his head like a Quentin Tarantino film until he was anticipating finding Emma covered in blood, with gangsters, heroin addicts and machine gun–toting thugs having some sort of underworld throw down over her body.

It wasn't a good train of thought.

What he did discover when he pulled into the lot was Emma tearing across the pavement, clearly illuminated by the streetlight, a thin girl chasing her. When she reached her car, she collided with the door and the assailant shoved her hard on her back, straight into the vehicle.

"Emma!" he screamed, throwing his car into Park in the middle of the lot. He shoved open the door and patted his pockets for his cell phone to call the cops as he took off in her direction, leaving his car running.

The girl fight was fairly standard, with lots of shrieking and exclamations of "You bitch!" along with hair pulling. Kyle didn't see any sign of weaponry on the stalker's part, but she was a scrappy little fighter, kicking Emma in the shins in a manner that made him wince as he reached them.

"Hey! Get off her." He wedged himself between the women, the element of surprise allowing him to disentangle their limbs without using any real force.

"Kyle! What are you doing here?" Emma asked, astonished.

"I was concerned," he told her wryly. "Clearly, I had reason to be." He braced his feet when Savannah pounded on his back and tried to get back to tearing Emma apart. He formed a cage with his arms around his insane girlfriend and tried to focus on the relief he felt that there was no bloodbath in the parking lot, just a crazy brunette. Along with a lunatic blonde.

He didn't want his back turned to either one, but the stalker scared him more than Emma's wild arm gestures. He whipped back around and assessed the woman in front of him, purposely backing Emma up to her car, so she was shielded by his body.

"I had everything under control," Emma protested, her head popping up over his shoulder.

He fought the urge to roll his eyes. "If this is under control, I'd hate to see out of control." Then he focused his attention on the stalker who was so angry she was twitching, her hands up and fingers arched like she was going to claw him. There was a definite lack of sanity in her expression.

"Savannah?" he asked.

She nodded.

"I suggest you back up slowly before I call the police." His first priority was getting the crazy girl away from Emma. They knew her name and contact information, so he wasn't worried about the police finding her. What he was worried about was the fact that Emma seemed intent on endangering herself. She was still trying to wiggle her way out from behind his back. He pushed his right leg between hers, pinning her.

"Hey!"

He ignored Emma and her protests.

Savannah had taken a step back and was eyeing him, clearly trying to assess the situation and calculate her best move. Probably realizing that he was the only witness and he'd seen her assaulting Emma, who had obviously been trying to get into her car, Savannah turned tail and ran.

Emma made a yelping sound. "Go after her!" she demanded, shoving against his back in an effort to dislodge him.

Kyle whirled on her and gripped both of her wrists. "Are you crazy?" he demanded, once he was sure Savannah was out of reach. With one eye on her as she climbed into a car parked on the opposite side of the lot, he resisted the urge to shake Emma. "What do you think you're doing? This isn't an art-museum gala where the only danger is eating a bad canapé. You agreed to meet a criminal in an empty parking lot!"

Her nose wrinkled, a sure sign she knew he was right. "I thought I could get her to confess, and I did." She dug into the pocket of her blazer and pulled out her phone. "I recorded it. I think."

That was not the sound of contrition. "Emma! What good does a confession do if you're dead?"

"She's not a murderer. She's just a wackadoodle."

"There's a difference? Not that I even know what a wackadoodle is."

Emma shoved on his chest again. "Will you back up? I can't breathe. She's gone so you can relax."

It was tempting to keep her immobile indefinitely, but he did step back a foot to give her air. "Do you have any idea how stupid this was? I can't even imagine what you thought was going to happen!"

"Exactly what did happen. I have enough information for Ian to get a restraining order against her." Emma was busy swiping and touching her phone, clearly checking her recording.

He heard the strains of voices talking as it played back. "You lied to me. No one knew where you were. You could have been seriously hurt." Was he the only one who realized that?

"Obviously someone did know where I was, since you found me. I told Sandy for safety purposes, not so she could rat me out to you." She made a face. "And I'm sorry for lying to you, but you would have tried to stop me."

"Uh, yeah. No shit." Now that his heart rate had

settled down into something resembling normal, he lifted his phone. "I'm calling the cops."

"Good." She nodded. "Savannah is clearly crazy. She needs to be stopped."

A normal woman would be rattled, but Emma looked oddly triumphant. It was more than a little disconcerting. "Why do you look so damn happy?"

"Because I possibly prevented a crime. That woman is on a path to really hurting someone. I was right. I listened to my gut and not Claire and now Savannah won't be able to walk in with a gun and start shooting at one of Ian's events. Because that's what I see going down eventually." She made the universal crazy gesture with her finger by her ear. "That chick is not right in the head."

"Neither are you," he said, still just so damn angry she had risked her own safety.

Her jaw dropped. "Excuse me?"

"Why didn't you just call the cops?"

"Maybe I wanted to hear what she had to say. Maybe I knew they would dismiss me. Maybe I needed more evidence. Or you know what?" Her voice rose. "Maybe I just had a lousy week because I got fired today while just recently my boyfriend got a promotion from the same boss. A stalker calling me a fat cow really was the punctuation point on a lousy week and it's just possible I wasn't thinking all that rationally. You should be supporting me, not standing there all high and mighty and criticizing me."

"You did this because of Claire? And why didn't you call me the second Claire laid you off? I had to find out from Sandy. Don't you trust me?"

"What? Of course I do. But it was humiliating to get fired!"

Kyle had known Claire's favoritism was going to be a problem between them. He didn't even hesitate. Life was too short, love too rare. "Do you want me to quit the paper? Because I'll do that."

"No!" She looked horrified at the prospect. "Absolutely not! If you do that, I'm just going to be a big bag of guilt and I could never live like that. I would hate myself."

Kyle suddenly had a gigantic headache. "So I'm supposed to keep the job so I can feel guilty?"

"You don't need to feel guilty."

He just stared at her, baffled. He had no idea where he was supposed to go from there. "Emma. Do you understand how much it hurts my feelings that you didn't trust me with the truth? If it weren't for Sandy telling me, would I even know? Were you ever going to tell me about arranging to meet Savannah?"

Her eyes dropping to the asphalt gave him his answer.

"You weren't, were you?"

"It was impulsive. I just got her email this afternoon. I would have told you I was contacting the police about Savannah. I might not have told you that I met up with her. Just to be totally honest. I might have left that part out."

She didn't even seem to understand how much that affected him. He was so angry and disappointed he just stood there and clenched his fists, swallowing hard. He needed a second to regroup.

"Hearing Claire say that I screwed up...having to walk out of the office in defeat, it was the worst thing ever. But maybe it really was for the best. I don't know what I'm going to do, but it's not going to be settling for the scraps Claire throws me off her dinner plate. I can do better than that."

Confidence was great and he was happy for her, but he also realized something with stunning clarity. "You really are a workaholic. I mean, what is the definition of a workaholic? Someone who prioritizes career over personal relationships, over personal well-being. Someone who lets their job consume both their waking and sleeping hours. Someone who can never disconnect themselves emotionally from that job. That's you."

Her face screwed up. "You're exaggerating. I don't do that. I spend every weekend with you."

It was a horrible realization, that Emma was wired in a way that meant ultimately, she was never going to see the world from his perspective. She would always put work first, despite the risks. The question was, could he live with that? He thought about his niece staring woefully up at him, and he knew that he wanted a family himself someday, with a woman who would be home before eight o'clock on weeknights. He wanted to enjoy his work, not be consumed by it, and he didn't want to be an afterthought to the woman he loved.

"Emma, you took off your top despite the fact that you would never in a million years do that if it hadn't been for work. You spent the entire summer focused on how to get a promotion and how to still secure the story you were told you couldn't have. You met a crazy woman in a dark parking lot. That's a workaholic." Throat tight, he leaned forward and kissed her on the forehead. "And I'm sorry, but I don't think I can be with you anymore. I don't want to be a pleasant afterthought to you. I want to be a priority. I want to enjoy life, not worry that you're working yourself to death like my dad did."

She blinked, tucking her hair behind her ear. "You're breaking up with me? Seriously?"

As much as he hated to, he realized it was what he needed to do before he fell even further in love with Emma. He knew he wouldn't be able to be happy. He would constantly be frustrated with her choices, and resent when she chose work over him.

"Yes. I'm sorry." He squeezed her hands, his voice gruff. "Now please get in the car and wait while I call the police. Are you sure you're not hurt?"

EMMA BLINKED AGAIN and again, taking short, urgent breaths so she wouldn't cry. Was she hurt? Was he seriously asking her that? "I'm fine." Which was a big fat lie. She might be fine physically, but Kyle had just emotionally sucker punched her.

Okay, so she had known he would be angry if he found out she'd met Savannah. She'd known he would be even angrier about her lying to him. It had been poor judgment on her part. But was that reason to break up with her? Talk about the ultimate punishment. Yes, she was a workaholic. They had established this. It wasn't front page news. It hadn't seemed to bother him the month and a half they had been dating, and she thought they had achieved a respectable balance between work and play.

So that just seemed like a convenient excuse to get out of the relationship.

Which made her wonder if something had gone down with Rosanna.

She didn't think it had—that just wasn't the kind of man Kyle was. But it was enough to cause her insecurities to leap to the surface and that pissed her off.

So she didn't say anything in protest. She didn't argue or defend herself or tell him she loved him. She simply got in her car and waited for the police, tears no longer threatening to fall, her mind and heart suddenly numb. That he would choose today of all days to break up with her was just brutal. It felt like she didn't even know him at all, because Kyle was normally very thoughtful and he was always there for her, or so she had thought.

Yes, she had done something monstrously stupid, but it had worked out in the end. She was confident she could have outrun Savannah. Everyone dealt with bad news in different ways, and Emma's was to take action. She didn't necessarily think that was a horrible thing, but Kyle clearly did. Just because his father had died of a heart attack in a hotel didn't mean she was destined to follow in his footsteps.

But they could have talked about it. He could have expressed his concerns and they could have had a rational conversation. Instead he had dumped her on what was arguably the worst day of her adult life. Nothing beat the embarrassment of having a bird poop on her head with an audience of fifty classmates on her first day of seventh grade, but today was a pretty close second.

When the cops arrived, she answered their questions carefully and thoroughly and told them everything she knew about Savannah. Kyle chimed in on occasion with additional information about the timeline and the original photo shoot.

Then it was over.

"Well, goodbye," she said, because what else was she supposed to say to Kyle? She would have been willing to apologize. In fact she'd tried, but then he had just dumped her, and her regret had been replaced with hurt and anger.

"Emma," he said, giving her a pleading look. "I'm sorry."

"Yeah," she said, her throat tight. "Me, too."

Then she got into her car and blindly headed toward the turnpike and home, tears flowing the second she was out of sight, thus unceremoniously ending the most important relationship of her adult life and by far the worst week ever. Not many people could say they lost both their job and their boyfriend in the same day. She was an overachiever that way.

Going home to an empty apartment, she realized she didn't even have a single person besides her mother she could call to go out for a drink with and lament and cry and bitch. And her mother was on a date with Buck. During the years since college she had lost touch with most of her girlfriends and saw them only on special occasions. Expecting them to drop everything and counsel her when she had screwed up was more than she could reasonably ask.

After a quick call to Sandy to tell her she was fine, Emma wasn't sure what else to do with herself.

"I'm sorry," Sandy said. "But I just felt like telling Kyle was the right thing to do."

"That's okay. I understand." She did, though she wasn't exactly thrilled about it. Emma kicked off her heels and flopped on her couch with a sigh. "And I appreciate the concern." There weren't a lot of people who cared about her, which was entirely her fault.

No one to blame for the utter silence of her apartment but herself.

You couldn't cuddle up with a byline. For the first time ever, Emma felt the full force of that revelation.

"He'll get over it," Sandy said, though she didn't sound all that sure of it.

"Thanks." Emma rubbed her sore feet and tried not to cry. "Keep in touch, okay?"

"Of course. We'll do lunch."

Emma was going to follow up on that. It was time to start nurturing friendships.

Once she was off the phone with Sandy, she poured herself a glass of wine, put on comfy pants, and texted and emailed every friend she'd ever had, while sobbing silently.

If her Friday night had a headline, it would be Sad Single Relies on Social Networking for Emotional Support.

As she flicked on the TV and waited for someone, anyone to respond to her, Emma pondered her future career options. Nun was looking like a real possibility.

Maybe she could be a professional Cautionary Tale.

But she suspected the pay for that wasn't that great.

And she was probably overqualified.

15

KYLE HELD HIS two-week-old niece, Jessica, and glared at his brother Andrew and his sister-in-law Katie. "You are both ruining this beautiful moment, you know. I'm bonding with Jessica and you're giving me crap."

"We're worried about you," Katie told him soothingly. His sister-in-law had morphed into the perfect picture of maternal calm, despite her obvious fatigue. She was serene, beautiful, natural with her daughter. Even the burping had gone away.

Andrew kept gazing at his wife with such naked admiration, Kyle was almost uncomfortable.

"You have enough going on without worrying about me," he told them sincerely, sitting in the lounge chair on the deck at his brother's, baby Jessica cradled in his arms. "I'm fine."

Which was a total lie, but he wasn't about to share that. He was miserable without Emma. He missed her fiercely.

His job was awful. He hated being on the front page, hated the pressure and the competition, and the rude questions he had to ask people who were in the midst of horrible life-changing events. He felt trapped, the life slowly being sucked out of him.

"Are you sure you can't work things out with your girl?" Andrew asked.

"I don't know." There was the rub. Kyle had gone around and around and he honestly didn't see how he could be happy with Emma being so career-centric. But he couldn't see how he was going to be happy without her, either. So basically he was screwed. Doomed to misery.

"You should call her."

"And say what? I can't ask her to change for me." Jessica gave a soft, delicate and soundless yawn, her round face a tiny picture of perfection. Looking down at her, he did know one thing—he wasn't going to waste another week of his life as Claire's toady, covering news that made him want to slit his wrists over the depravity of humanity. He was going to quit first thing Monday. With a recommendation that Emma be hired for his position.

He did exactly that, despite Claire's blustering and protests. He held firm, and told her she would be wise to hire Emma back on staff. Maybe he couldn't be with Emma, but he absolutely wanted her to be happy and doing her dream job.

"Are you sure you don't want me to reassign you? Sports can find a place for you."

"No. I think I'm ready for the next chapter in my life," he told Claire truthfully. He wasn't entirely sure what that was going to be, but he had been fairly frugal with his spending and he had decent savings set aside. "So are you going to offer Emma the job?"

She shrugged. "I'll consider it." Then she smiled,

her red fingernails sliding across her neck, down to rest at the peak of her nonexistent cleavage. "Well, if you're serious about this, then one good thing can come out of it."

"What's that?" Though he had a horrible suspicion of where she was headed.

"You and I can have naughty, dirty sex. I like to be tied up," she told him with a wink.

He would like to say that Claire was a nice enough woman, or that he respected her as a boss, or even that she had a soft side under her tough exterior. But he couldn't say any of those things, because frankly, she was just a bitch, and was probably selfish and demanding in bed. Not his type at all, under any circumstances, and certainly not under these.

"I appreciate the offer," he lied, his tone casual. "But I'm going to go solo for a while." Determined to help Emma, though, he added, "I'll have Sandy let Emma know you'll be contacting her."

"You're not going to tell her yourself?" Her eyes were shrewd, her voice sharp.

"No. I haven't spoken to her in several weeks."

"Interesting. Sure, maybe I'll call her. If you agree to go out for a drink with me."

She wasn't playing around. Kyle took the bait, because he knew how much this job meant to Emma. "One drink. No sex. And you offer her the front page position without telling her we discussed it."

"Done." Claire stood and shook his hand. "It's been a pleasure working with you. Don't bother with the two weeks, go ahead and clear out your desk this afternoon, and I'll see you tonight at the wine and martini bar on 117th Street."

She was nothing if not efficient.

Kyle nodded and went out to pack up his entire newspaper career.

EMMA SAT IN FRONT of her computer, staring at the mock-up news page she had created using a template. The name of her fake paper was *Emma's Extra! Extra!* The first headline read Woman Miserable Without Her Boyfriend.

The article described the misery she had genuinely been feeling since Kyle had left her in that parking lot, then continued with what she hoped was a touch of humor that he would enjoy.

Emma Gideon has been suffering the worst kind of regret for her poor choices and her misplaced priorities. One can only be left to ponder what will happen as she slides into old age, pining for her one true love, Kyle Hadley. Who happens to be hot.

Unemployed Journalist Finds Job Helping Other Unemployed Women.

Emma Gideon accepts position with nonprofit committed to the training of unemployed women and single mothers in need, as well as providing them with clothing for professional interviews. Ms. Gideon is looking forward to growing the agency and serving as many women as possible.

Sign-Up Still Open For Swing Dancing Lessons— Must Have Partner.

Karaoke Contest This Friday at Lucky's.

Then of course, the personal ad:

SWF reformed workaholic seeks SWM for long walks with dachshunds and a no-pressure relation-

ship. Enjoys karaoke, steamed broccoli, frozen fruit bars and long hot showers with green men.

Biting her fingernails, Emma scanned it one more time for typos, but didn't find any. She had put her picture in the upper left-hand corner, a shot of her with a tremendous amount of cleavage exposed, a pencil suggestively between her teeth. She'd had Sandy snap the picture, which had taken a good twenty failed attempts to capture as they both had kept laughing hysterically.

Knowing it was now or never, she hit Send and gave a sigh of relief. If she didn't hear back from Kyle, then she would know it was truly over, but she had to at least try to get him to talk to her. Hence the newspaper. She figured if anything, he would get some amusement out of it.

She did have tremendous regret for her missteps. The broken heart aside, several positives had come out of Kyle's dumping her in a much-needed wake-up call. Her desperate night of texting and emailing had resulted in her making plans with half a dozen friends she hadn't seen in ages, and the agreed-upon lunch with Sandy. She also had been highly motivated to get a job doing something she loved and which would have a positive impact on the community, without demanding sixty-hour workweeks. Fortunately, her existing work with a nonprofit that trained single mothers had given her an edge, and she was thrilled she had been hired on as full-time staff.

Life would go on if Kyle wasn't interested in rekindling their relationship.

But she'd be much happier if he was.

Her cell phone rang and she jumped in her chair, heart in her throat. Was it Kyle?

A glance at the screen had her frowning. Gross. It was Claire. The last person she wanted to talk to, especially since she'd like to think that Kyle would get her email and call her instantly, and she did not want to be on the phone with her former boss and miss his call.

She almost hit Ignore, but she was curious as to what Claire wanted. It was a Wednesday night and there was no reason for Claire to be contacting her at all, let alone outside of work hours.

"Hello?"

"Hey, Emma, it's Claire. How are you?"

"Fine, thanks. You?" Not that she cared how Claire was. She rolled her eyes at the inane niceties between them.

"Good. Listen, there's been a reshuffle here at the paper and if you want it, you can have the byline for page one."

"What?" she gasped. "What happened to Kyle? I thought he was the new page-one guy."

"He quit. He suggested I give the position to you."

"Why would he do that?" she asked, astonished.

"How the hell should I know?" Claire asked irritably. "Do you want the job or not? There's a martini with my name on it and I'm getting impatient."

Ironically, she was being offered the job she had lusted after for almost three years and she no longer wanted it.

"Thank you, Claire. I appreciate the offer, but I'm going to have to decline. I've already accepted another position."

"With whom?"

"A nonprofit."

"Are you kidding me? So you're just going to ditch your career at the paper? After all I've done for you?"

Yeah, firing her. That's what Claire had done for her. But Emma no longer felt any animosity toward her old boss. In the end, she had made some incredibly positive changes in her life, and if Claire hadn't fired her, she wasn't sure she would have ever made those adjustments. At least not anytime soon.

"I'm sorry, but yes, I'm ready for something different." The relief she felt in saying that, and meaning it, was enormous.

"You're both insane. God, I'm so glad I'm not in my twenties anymore."

With that, Claire hung up.

Emma laughed. Then she put down her phone and stared at her in-box. Nothing. She glanced at her phone. Nothing.

After twenty minutes, she forced herself to shut off her computer and put on a movie to distract herself. A watched cell phone never rings.

She was barely into the BBC version of *Pride and Prejudice,* wondering if it would be wrong to fast-forward to the scene where Colin Firth emerged from the water, when her phone buzzed. Mercy, it was Kyle texting her.

So I got the news. Congrats!

Thanks.

Debating whether she should elaborate on that or not, she bit her bottom lip and pleaded for him to say more. "Please, please, please want to be with me."

SWM seeks SWF to forgive him for being an asshole.

Relief had her giddy, giggling on her couch.

Done. SWM had a point.

SWM missed SWF and wants to come upstairs.

Then he added:

I'm in your parking lot. I love you, Emma.

Score. Emma's heart surged.

I love you, too.

Then she ran across her apartment, threw open the door, and jogged down the three flights of stairs, disregarding the fact she was barefoot and wearing nothing but pajama shorts and a tank top without a bra. He was already on the landing when she got there, and she ran straight into his arms.

He picked her up and swung her around. "I'm so sorry," he murmured, kissing her. "I was a jerk. I mean, of all the days to break up, that was the worst."

She kissed him back with all the excitement and passion she felt for the future, and with all the regret she had for the mistakes she'd made. "I'm sorry, too, for lying, for mixing up my priorities."

"Let's try this again."

"Sounds good to me."

Kyle grinned at her, squeezing her tightly. "Let's go give *Emma's Extra! Extra!* a new headline."

She shivered in anticipation, happiness settling over her. "Like what?"

"How about Woman Strips for Boyfriend?" He raised his eyebrows up and down.

"I think that's a good start," she told him.

Then she leaned forward and whispered her suggestion of a follow-up story.

Emma laughed when his jaw dropped in shock.

"*Damn.* That is newsworthy," Kyle agreed. "Good thing I ate my Wheaties today."

Kyle took her hand and tugged her toward her apartment. He seemed as desperate as she did to meld her body with his, as eager to show her how much he had missed her.

"Since I'm no longer a workaholic, I may just lie there and let you do all the hard stuff," she told him with a grin.

"Fine by me. Nice picture, by the way. I like the cleavage."

"You're welcome," she told him, very sassily.

Kyle laughed. "You have no idea what you're in for. "Woman Dies from Oral Sex Overload."

"At least I'll die happy," she told him, closing the door of her apartment behind them.

Kyle cupped her cheeks in his hands and said in all seriousness, "You make me very, very happy. I love you."

"I love you, too." Emma turned her head and kissed his hand. "Now get naked."

"Do I have to sign a waiver?" he joked.

"Yes, promising me your firstborn."

"Well, that'll work," he murmured, his hands brushing over the ribbon of skin exposed above her shorts. "Because I'm hoping it will be yours, too."

And he kissed her to put an exclamation mark on it.

* * * * *

Look for the next book in the
FROM EVERY ANGLE *series*
by Erin McCarthy!
Available in October 2014
from Harlequin Blaze.

Available July 15, 2014

#807 RIDING HOME
Sons of Chance
by Vicki Lewis Thompson
Zach Powell has left the law for ranch life. He's just the cowboy to help perfectionist lawyer Jeannette Trenton learn to forgive herself—and let loose. But one wild weekend isn't enough to satisfy their desire....

#808 DARE ME
It's Trading Men!
by Jo Leigh
Wine expert Molly Webster craves the finer things in life, but one taste of master brewer Cameron Crawford sends her into sensory overload. Too bad their chemistry can only last one night!

#809 COMMAND CONTROL
Uniformly Hot!
by Sara Jane Stone
Erotica writer Sadie Bannerman is just looking for one good man...who doesn't mind being tied up. And dangerously hot Army Ranger Logan Reed is reporting for duty!

#810 THE MIGHTY QUINNS: ROGAN
The Mighty Quinns
by Kate Hoffmann
Straight-laced psychologist Claudia Mathison is determined to unearth sexy adventure guide Rogan Quinn's deepest secrets. But Rogan figures the best way to keep her out of his head is to keep her *in* his bed.

YOU CAN FIND MORE INFORMATION ON UPCOMING HARLEQUIN® TITLES, FREE EXCERPTS AND MORE AT WWW.HARLEQUIN.COM.

HBCNM0714

REQUEST YOUR FREE BOOKS!
2 FREE NOVELS PLUS 2 FREE GIFTS!

red-hot reads!

YES! Please send me 2 FREE Harlequin® Blaze™ novels and my 2 FREE gifts (gifts are worth about $10). After receiving them, if I don't wish to receive any more books, I can return the shipping statement marked "cancel." If I don't cancel, I will receive 4 brand-new novels every month and be billed just $4.74 per book in the U.S. or $4.96 per book in Canada. That's a savings of at least 14% off the cover price. It's quite a bargain. Shipping and handling is just 50¢ per book in the U.S. and 75¢ per book in Canada.* I understand that accepting the 2 free books and gifts places me under no obligation to buy anything. I can always return a shipment and cancel at any time. Even if I never buy another book, the two free books and gifts are mine to keep forever.

150/350 HDN F4WC

Name	(PLEASE PRINT)

Address	Apt. #

City	State/Prov.	Zip/Postal Code

Signature (if under 18, a parent or guardian must sign)

Mail to the Harlequin® Reader Service:
IN U.S.A.: P.O. Box 1867, Buffalo, NY 14240-1867
IN CANADA: P.O. Box 609, Fort Erie, Ontario L2A 5X3

Want to try two free books from another line?
Call 1-800-873-8635 or visit www.ReaderService.com.

* Terms and prices subject to change without notice. Prices do not include applicable taxes. Sales tax applicable in N.Y. Canadian residents will be charged applicable taxes. Offer not valid in Quebec. This offer is limited to one order per household. Not valid for current subscribers to Harlequin Blaze books. All orders subject to credit approval. Credit or debit balances in a customer's account(s) may be offset by any other outstanding balance owed by or to the customer. Please allow 4 to 6 weeks for delivery. Offer available while quantities last.

Your Privacy—The Harlequin® Reader Service is committed to protecting your privacy. Our Privacy Policy is available online at www.ReaderService.com or upon request from the Harlequin Reader Service.

We make a portion of our mailing list available to reputable third parties that offer products we believe may interest you. If you prefer that we not exchange your name with third parties, or if you wish to clarify or modify your communication preferences, please visit us at www.ReaderService.com/consumerschoice or write to us at Harlequin Reader Service Preference Service, P.O. Box 9062, Buffalo, NY 14269. Include your complete name and address.

SPECIAL EXCERPT FROM

HARLEQUIN

Blaze

Enjoy a sizzling sneak peek of

Command Control

by Sara Jane Stone—the latest in the
reader-favorite *Uniformly Hot!* miniseries!

After more than a decade in the army, Logan knew when to withdraw and wait for the enemy to pass. Opening the door to Main Street Books, he slipped inside. He found a position deep in the maze of bookshelves. Pulling the nearest book from the shelf, he pretended to read the back cover.

"If you need assistance picking out a romance novel, I can help."

His gaze snapped to the redhead standing two feet away. The desire he'd felt when he'd seen her the day before returned full force.

"But if it's your first time—" she continued "—you might want to steer clear of erotica."

"Erotica?" Logan glanced at the book in his hand. On the front cover was a practically nude woman lying on a bed. A man in leather pants stood next to her holding a whip. Not what he'd expect to find on the shelf in his hometown. "Mount Pleasant sells erotica?"

"Not much," she said grimly. "But what they do have is pretty good."

She stepped toward him and reached for a book on the shelf above his head. The side of her breast brushed his arm, sending a red-alert signal through his body.

"If you're looking for a classic romance, this is one of my favorites." She held out a copy of a Jane Austen novel.

HBEXP79813

He shook his head. "Read that one in high school. It wasn't for me."

She placed the book on the shelf and turned to him, her eyes sparkling with amusement. "To find the perfect romance, I'll need to know a little bit more about you."

"Not much to tell. I'm home on leave."

"You're a soldier?" Her smile widened. "Let me guess. Special Forces."

"Army ranger."

"No kidding?" Laughing, she scanned the shelves before selecting another paperback. "This one should be just right for you."

She handed him the book. The cover showed a man with a naked chest, dog tags hanging around his neck.

"He's a SEAL, and she's a nurse," she said. "They have hot sex, overcome a few challenges and fall in love."

"The hot sex part sounds good." He set the book back on the shelf. "But I'm not looking for a fairy-tale ending."

She handed him back the first book. "Then maybe you should stick with erotica."

Her fingers touched his and lingered. He glanced up at her and saw the heat in her eyes. Whatever was happening here wasn't one-sided. He shook his head. "I'm not into whips."

"What if I told you I could convince you to give it a try?"

"Are you really into—"

"No, I was teasing. Whips aren't my thing," she said, smiling. "And I'm Sadie."

"Logan." He ran a hand over the back of his neck. "But now I'm curious how you'd convince me…."

Pick up COMMAND CONTROL by Sara Jane Stone, on sale August 2014 wherever Harlequin® Blaze® books and ebooks are sold.

Saddle up for a wild ride!

Zach Powell has left the law for ranch life. He's just the cowboy to help perfectionist lawyer Jeannette Trenton learn to forgive herself—and let loose. But one wild weekend isn't enough to satisfy their desire....

Don't miss the final chapter of the *Sons of Chance* trilogy

Riding Home

from *New York Times* bestselling author

Vicki Lewis Thompson

Available August 2014 wherever you buy Harlequin Blaze books.

HARLEQUIN®

Blaze®

Red-Hot Reads
www.Harlequin.com

HB79811